Send *Her* ~~to~~

MW00916255

Edition License Notes

Send *Her* to Me Lord

By Khara Campbell

Synopsis:

There comes a time in everyone's life when they stop to evaluate their goals, priorities, and the people in their circle. Thirty-six-year-old Malik Day is no different. He has come to realize "doing the same thing over and over and expecting a different outcome" is truly insanity. It is time he mans up and get his life in order. One of the top things on his list is finding a godly wife. However, God doesn't always bless us with the package we expect.

"There is no fear in love, but perfect love casts out fear. For fear has to do with punishment, and whoever fears has not been perfected in love." 1 John 4:18

WARNING

This book contains some topics that may be sensitive for some. If the topic of miscarriage is a trigger for you, you may want to bypass this book.

1

MALIK

"Yeah, you need to leave with ya broke behind! I'm the breadwinner…me! I make sure all the bills are paid. All you do is bring home petty cash you make cutting grass and power washing." Janae throws insults at me which, unfortunately, is nothing new. And I have stupidly put up with it for four years.

Love.

I shake my head while picking up a pair of my work pants she hauled at me from the bedroom. I stuff it in a trash bag along with the other articles of clothing and shoes on the hallway hardwood floor.

I'm only making petty cash now because business has been frustratingly slow for over a year. The government shutdown months ago made matters worse. People are really tight with their money right now. But you would think my fiancée would understand that. Understand that her man is busting his butt every day to rebuild his clientele and hire two helpers like he had before.

Like I had when we met four years ago. When my yearly gross income from the business was $150,000 – when I had two work trucks and two men working part-time on payroll. When, after Janae and I had been together for a year, I paid for her to go back to school to become a dental hygienist. Now she's making a steady income of $60K a year and, because my yearly income has dropped to about $35K, in her eyes, I'm now a bum.

I'm done with this. I shove my things in the bag, trying my best to ignore Janae as she continues showing all the way out, throwing my clothes and shoes.

"A woman needs more than a warm body in her bed every night. Here we were supposed to be planning our wedding and you can't even afford to pay for the dress I want..."

The dress she wants cost ten grand. For her to wear one day for maybe four hours.

"...And I always dreamt of going to Hawaii for my honeymoon, but you can't afford that either..."

But before my business started to struggle, I was able to save sixty thousand for a down payment for our first house. She definitely doesn't need to know that now. I had planned to tell her that on our wedding night a year from now.

"...As a man you're supposed to be able to provide for me. Then you come home tonight telling me we can't take our bae cation to Vegas. Not the Bahamas or Italy, or Fiji. Vegas! Going to Vegas is cheap as hell and you can't even afford that. I'm so sick of you. You're thirty-six with nothing to show for yourself. We live in an apartment. People our age should be on their second houses by now. But I'm gonna do me and build on my own. I'm done carrying you on my back."

I have nothing to say to her. I should have been gone. Been left this toxic relationship. I refuse to repeatedly defend myself to a woman who's supposed to love and support me unconditionally. I met her when she was thirty-two, with less than a hundred dollars in her bank account. She had resigned herself to making a career of being a waitress at Waffle House, where I met her.

I had come in to inquire with the manager about doing their landscaping. She was the first person I noticed when I walked in. Her box braids had a lot of new growth and were begging to be taken down. But Janae's natural beauty overshadowed her bad hair day. When I walked into the restaurant, she greeted me with a bright smile, and I had been a goner for her since. But no more. I'm done!

"You're not going to say anything?" Janae shouts.

I sigh deeply then finally turn my head towards her. Her mocha skin and size ten frame do nothing for me anymore. Her attitude killed all that. Looking her in the eyes, I shake my head. I haul the full, extra-large trash bag on my back and start to walk down the hall.

"That's it? You have nothing to say, Malik? Four years and you have nothing to say?" She sucks her teeth. "I can't believe I wasted my time with you. You have done nothing for me! Nothing! Broke ass!"

It takes every fiber of my being not to go postal on her.

There is a God.

I make it to the front door of the apartment without saying a word. I'll come back tomorrow when she's at work to clear out the rest of my things. I hope she doesn't do anything stupid with them before then.

Thirty-three minutes later, I pull into the driveway of my brother's house in Fort Washington, Maryland. Drew is older than me by four years. He's the only family I've got. Our parents died nine years ago in a boating accident in Florida.

"Dude, why are you bringing trash in my house?" Drew hollers at me after I make my way into the kitchen from the door that leads to the garage.

"What's up, Uncle Malik?" Kason, my thirteen-year-old nephew asks. He looks so much like my brother, which means he looks so much like me with his dark complexion and faded haircut that all three of us sport. Whenever he and I are out together, people think he's my son.

I have always wanted children – at least one. I'm so thankful Janae was so adamant about waiting for marriage to have kids. I dodged a bullet, not having her as a baby mama.

I set the trash bag filled with my clothes down on the tiled kitchen floor. "My clothes are in the bag," I tell my brother who is standing at the counter cutting what looks and smells like lasagna.

"I'm good, Kason, how's school?" I sit next to him on the vacant stool at the counter.

"School's good," he tells me.

Drew clears his throat looking over at his son.

Kason gives it to me straight. "Actually, school could be better if I could get my History and English grades up."

"That's 'cause his mind be on those damn video games all day." My sister-in-law, Deidre, walks into the kitchen. "You came to mooch food again, Malik?" she teases me.

She's a beautiful, honey-toned woman with a Bohemian style. She and Drew are both accountants, running their own accounting firm. They make sure my business accounts stay in the black.

"I'm not the one to wish doom on anyone's relationship, but Janae is not wifey material. She can't cook. Don't clean. And I'll just leave it at that, cause there's more. You can do so much better." Deidre sits at the kitchen counter on the side with her husband. Drew has four plates with huge pieces of lasagna with tossed salad on the side.

"You're right. Janae isn't wife material and she just kicked me out of the apartment that I lease. Good thing it's a month-to-month lease. I'll be looking for a new place to live. So, for the time being, is it okay if I crash here?"

All three of them look at me in shock.

"Are you for real? The witch is gone? No more Malik and Janae?" Deidre asks dramatically.

"Bro, you serious? As many times as I told you to leave that girl...four years to be exact. You aren't pranking us, right?"

"Y'all hated her that much?" I ask them.

"Uncle Malik, I know I may not be old enough to understand all the workings of a grown up relationship, but suffice it to say, my parents just may throw you a party now that you and Janae aren't together. I was never quite fond of her myself."

My mouth drops open in shock and amazement. "How are you failing English when you can talk like that?"

Deidre points her finger over at her son. "Exactly! I did not raise any fool. And Kason knows those grades better get right real quick. He too busy checking for them fast tail lil' girls."

"I thought it was the video games that was distracting him," Drew smirks.

Kason tries to hide his laugh.

"Whatever. But back to you," Deidre gives me a pointed look. "When shall we have the 'Malik is free from Janae' party?"

I grimace. I don't know if I should laugh or be ashamed that I didn't leave Janae sooner. In my defense, she wasn't like this in the beginning. Coldhearted. Selfish. Materialistic. Instagram likes Junkie.

Maybe because she played nice until she used you and sucked the money and joy right out of your life.

Ever since my business, Precise Cuts Landscaping, started experiencing a drop in sales, Janae has been giving me the stink eye. Money isn't coming in as quickly as it used to. I had lost my contract with a local grocery store chain that sold out to another company. The new company had no interest in working with me. Which meant I lost the biggest egg in my financial basket.

I made a vow then to secure more than one major contract, so I wouldn't be in this predicament again. It's been over a year and I haven't been able to secure any major deals. But I'm thankful for my residential jobs. They take care of my essential financial obligations. *Thank You, Jesus.*

I had come home to our apartment earlier and told Janae it wasn't a smart financial move for us to take a trip to Vegas next month because after I took care of my business expenses – and despite her saying she paid all the bills in the house – after *I* paid the rent and light bill, there wasn't much left to spend on a trip.

Being the man, I didn't ask Janae for a dime of her money. I made sure the bills were paid. I'm not prideful. If she offered, I wouldn't mind the help, but I still feel it's my responsibility. She's never offered.

Janae does make sure the apartment is filled with groceries. Because she can't eat anything unless it's organic. I have absolutely nothing against organic food – other than it being ridiculously expense. It's just an example of how much Janae has changed in the four years we've been together. She didn't even know what eating organic was...

You know what? I'm not going to bash her. It hurts that in my low moments, she never reached out to support me. Held her man down. A faithful man that made sure *all* her needs were met. It is what it is. We didn't work out. The end.

"No need for a party. But yes, Janae and I are done! I'm going to wait until she's at work tomorrow so I can get the rest of my stuff. But y'all still ain't said if I can stay here for a while. I mean y'all do have two extra bedrooms."

"Yeah, you can stay." Drew hands me my plate of food.

"Thanks. Just give me a couple weeks to find me a new apartment." I pick up my fork to dive into my lasagna and salad.

Deidre smacks my hand. "You know we pray in this house. Matter of fact, since you're staying here for a couple weeks, come to church with us on Sunday."

"Sure." I'm one of those Christians that doesn't go to church. There's no particular reason why, other than I'm either working a job on Sunday or there's a football game to watch.

We gather hands to pray. Looking at my brother and his family – I realize I want this. A loving wife, an awesome son that looks like me, a beautiful home, and God at the center.

Send her to me, Lord.

I know I need to work on me and prepare myself for whoever she may be.

Deidre prays. "Dear Jehovah God, thank You for this day. Thank You that my brother-in-law is no longer sleeping with the devil…"

I bite my lip to stop from laughing.

"Thank You for family. Thank You for Your many blessings. Thank You for this food we're about to eat, may it do our bodies good, in Jesus' name..."

We all say, "Amen."

My cellphone vibrates in my pocket. I pull it out discreetly to see a text message from Janae. Will it be easy to let her go?

2

RAE

"You can't keep a damn thing, Rae!" Greg roars. "You couldn't keep none of our babies in your womb long enough, you couldn't keep a job and you for damn sure couldn't keep me."

I watch him haphazardly fling his clothing out of the walk-in closet into the suitcase he had thrown on the floor.

"I can't wait for our divorce to be final. Thanks to your dried-up womb, us having no kids makes the process easier. You can keep this house and your car and I don't even mind paying you your lousy one thousand a month in spousal support, cause you're working now so I won't have to pay that for long. As long as I'm no longer tied to you in marriage, I'm good." Done with gathering his things, Greg zips up the suitcase, lifts it up then starts for the bedroom door.

Greg and I met after I moved to Maryland from a small town in North Carolina. After college I had moved back home to Beaufort, but work as a pharmacist there wasn't financially rewarding. And I was ready for a change of scenery from the mundane. Even my parents had sold my childhood home and moved to Myrtle Beach, leaving me behind.

I moved to Maryland after I landed a job with a popular pharmacy chain and rented a two-bedroom condo in Upper Marlboro, Maryland. Greg was my next-door neighbor and offered to help me with my boxes when he saw me unloading my Jeep Wrangler. If I had known then what I know now, I would have run far away from him.

He was charming from the start. He helped me haul all my boxes and when the moving truck came with my furniture, he assisted me with setting everything up. Greg was a complete stranger and it may not have been wise for me to have him all up in my new condo. I appreciated his help though, because I needed it. He also didn't give off any "deranged criminal" vibe so I felt comfortable trusting him so quickly.

From that day on, we spent all our free time together. Greg is an auditor with the federal government and made it his mission to be my personal DC, Maryland and Virginia tri-state guide while I got accustomed to my new surroundings. He was my only companion in my new city. It didn't hurt that he was gorgeous. Tall and light skinned with pink, kissable lips. His confidence was the icing on the cake. He owned every room he walked into and people took notice.

After six months of dating, Greg asked for my hand in marriage. Six months later we were husband and wife. The first year of marriage was absolute bliss...then I got pregnant and suffered my first miscarriage. Now here we are.

Sitting cross-legged in the middle of the bed, I watch him with tears burning the back of my eyes. I refuse to let them fall in front of him. My marriage of six years is officially over. I could never give my husband the one thing he wanted most from me - kids. And my lack of keeping a job was because I've been pregnant five times in six years.

At thirty-nine years old, I've come to – or I'm still trying to – accept that my desire to be a mother will never be fulfilled. From my third miscarriage, I was considered high-risk for pregnancy and placed on strict restrictions, meaning my job as a pharmacist, standing on my feet for the majority of the day was a no-no. I never kept any pregnancy beyond three months. Each loss of a child chipped away at something deep inside of me. I feel as worthless as my very soon-to-be ex-husband makes me feel.

I refuse to let him see me cry – *anymore*.

"You're not gonna say anything?" Greg asks, looking over his shoulder at me with a sneer.

I glance over to look at his light skinned face and pink lips. *What the hell does he expect me to say? Stay? Hell, no!*

He shakes his head, pitying me. I hate that the most about him. From most people, actually, that feel my lack of birthing a child makes me less than. I'm my own worst enemy in that category, so it infuriates me when others pity me.

But I'm not going to give Greg the satisfaction of getting a reaction out of me. *No more!*

"I don't know why I expected you to fight for me. You're nothing like the woman I married six years ago." He cuts his eyes away from me, shaking his head in disgust, then exits the bedroom.

"I'm no longer the woman you married because you slowly killed and robbed me of my self-esteem, hope and love." I whisper to his retreating back.

When I hear the front door slam shut, then his car starting and driving off, I finally let the dam break. Tears drench my face.

God, why? Why have You blessed me to conceive so many babies but never to give life to them?

I'm asking for myself, not because it would have made Greg stay. But because at least now with Greg gone, I would've had the comfort of my child.

Why give a woman a womb and not bless her to hold her alive healthy baby in her arms? Why God? Why would You do this to me?

I've asked God this too many times to count. I have always wanted children. Being an only child, I had dreamt of being a mother of at least four kids. Each pregnancy, though I had suffered a loss prior, I had hope. Hope that the miracle inside of me would birth to life. I have not allowed doctors to poke and prod me to find out why I keep losing my babies because I don't need the obvious confirmed, my body has made it abundantly clear. I'm not meant to give birth. Some things don't need to be explained by science.

Despite why I lost all my babies, I place my trust, faith and hope in Jehovah. One day, I will come to peace with it all. I'm one hundred percent certain without my faith I would've gone insane. Losing five babies is not for the faint of heart. Some days I handle it well – but then there are those days when I just want to crawl under a rock and die. Today is one of those days.

The Scripture Jeremiah 29:11 plays like a loop in my mind…*"For I know the plans I have for you,"* declares the Lord, *"plans to prosper you and not to harm you, plans to give you hope and a future."*

I lay my head on my pillow, falling asleep with a tear-stained face and God's Word whispering in my mind.

What will become of my life now?

3

MALIK

It's been two days since Janae kicked me out of my own apartment and I'm feeling better today than I have in months. Drew and Deidre were right – Janae was sucking the life out of me. I feel like a bird finally let free from its cage. My money is still funny but I'm healthy, in my right mind and I have my brother and his family on my side. God is good.

I place my truck in park just as my cellphone chirps in the cup holder. My Chevy pickup doubles as my work and personal vehicle. I just finished a biweekly residential job and now I'm picking up some things Drew asked me to get on my way home. I look at the text message, shaking my head. *The devil is always busy.*

Janae: So, you dodging my calls now Malik? When are you coming home? Let me find out you at a bitch house.

Seconds later…

Janae: I can't stand you! Stay with that hoe! You worthless anyway. I have men begging for my attention all the time, and guess what? I'm about to give them all my time. I had a fine-looking investment broker in my chair today, after I cleaned his teeth, he asked me for my number, and I gave it to him. Guess I'm about to upgrade.

I shake my head while going through the steps to block her number from my phone. *I can't believe I put up with that for four years.*

I get out of my truck and make my way inside the black-owned pharmacy Drew and Deidre boast about. I have to pick up Kason's eczema medication. I look over the aisles in the small store, making my way towards the pharmacy counter.

The first person I notice in the pharmacy section is a beautiful, brown-skinned woman, about a size eight, in a lab coat. She has her hair up in a big, glorious afro-puff that makes me what to put up my fist in a black power sign. Large, gold hoop earrings hang from her ears and a sparkle of a thin gold chain with a script pendant around her neck. I cannot quite make out what it reads. I probably can when I get closer.

God, you did mighty good with this one, I think stepping closer to the counter. If I was ready to get back into a relationship, I would shoot my shot. I'm not. I need time alone to get my life in order. Strengthen my relationship with the Lord. Going to church on Sunday with my brother and his family has me excited.

"Good evening, I'm here to pick up a prescription for Kason Day." I flash her a smile. I may not shoot my shot, but harmless flirting doesn't hurt.

She gives me a professional smile that doesn't reach her eyes. But the smile is still pleasant and for reasons unknown to me now, I have an urge to bring out the natural smile that would light up her beautiful, makeup-free face. Her pendant reads 1980 and if that perhaps is her birth year, that would mean she's forty or will be turning forty this year. She looks much younger – younger than me. My birthday is next month and I'll be thirty-seven. Again, if I was interested in shooting my shot, her being three years older than me wouldn't mean a thing.

"I recall that name. I believe I left a message an hour ago about it being ready for pick up. Give me a sec." She walks away and goes to the alphabetically labeled shelves to retrieve the prescription.

Forgive me, Lord, but I can't help checking her out from behind. *Good God*. Okay, I'm not looking any more. I avert my eyes from her ample, perfectly-shaped derriere that her lab coat does a poor job of hiding to look at the magazine rack below the counter.

She comes back to the counter with the prescription cream in a white paper bag. "Here you go, sir. I just need you to sign for it."

"Do I have to pay for it up front?" There's a cashier at the front of the store.

"I think it's covered by insurance. If not, you can pay here."

I watch her as she scans the barcode on the bag. She has five beauty marks on her face. The one on her right cheek is my favorite. I read the name on her lab coat, Dr. Rae Cooper. I know nothing about this woman. She could have a man and kids at home for all I know. But I make a vow to myself to come back and find her when I get my life in order.

Rae peels off a sticker with a barcode and places it in a book. "Sign here, please." She points to the line, handing me a pen. "And the prescription is fully covered under insurance."

I sign where she indicated. "Are you the owner?"

"No. Dr. Dean worked the morning shift. She'll be back tomorrow afternoon."

"Okay. I own a landscaping business. Do you know if she's looking for someone to take care of the lawn?" I ask, hopeful, though from what I saw, the lawn looks taken care of.

"I'm sorry, no. Her nephew takes care of the lawn."

"Okay. It didn't hurt to ask."

Rae hands me the bag with the eczema cream. "I think you may have better luck at Judea's Bakery in Accokeek. It's too big of a job for Dr. Dean's nephew to handle since he's a senior in high school and can't keep up with the maintenance. Tell Judea, the owner, that Pharmacist Rae sent you."

I smile big. "Thank you. I appreciate it."

She gives me a smile that reaches her eyes this time. "You're welcome."

I leave the pharmacy feeling ten feet tall.

I really need to get my life in check so I can come back to shoot my shot.

4

RAE

"Who was that God's gift to mankind?" Yasmine asks from behind me. She's one of the pharmacy assistants on staff and my favorite to work with since I have been here for seven months. She's a bi-racial chick in her late twenties and keeps me up to date with what's going on with the culture. I don't even have an Instagram page, which in her eyes makes me an abnormality. I had covered for her at the counter while she took a restroom break.

"Just another customer." I move away from the counter to continue filling prescriptions. We have two more hours before the store closes at 8pm. I love working here. First of all, it's woman and black owned. Secondly, I don't have to work late hours. My previous jobs at chain pharmacies were murder to my social life. Not that I have a social life. But it's great not having to sometimes work until 10pm at night on shift. The downside to that is not having anyone to go home to.

I shake my head to rid my train of thoughts. No need going down that rabbit hole.

"He was fione! Dark chocolate, full beard, bedroom eyes…"

I look over at Yasmine. "How did you notice all of that?"

"I can spot a fine man miles away. And you haven't denied my description of him either."

'Cause she's right.

He's gorgeous. And the way he was watching me like I was the best thing he'd ever seen was unnerving. But a man is the last thing I need right now. I'm still married. My divorce won't be final for another month. I need alone time to heal. Heal from a marriage to a heartless man and heal from being barren.

"Let's just say if I had met him seven years ago, I would ask him out in a heartbeat." Because strangely, from the brief encounter I had with him, he seemed like the kind of man you don't let slip through your fingers.

"That's what I'm talking about. Brotha had that, *'I'll build you a house, crack your back and worship you like a goddess'* vibe going on."

Again, she's right.

My cellphone vibrates in my lab coat pocket. I pull it out. My mother's name shows on the screen. "Yasmine, I'm going to take a fifteen-minute break."

"Okay," she says over her shoulder.

I answer the call from my mom as I make my way to the small breakroom. "Hey mom."

"Rae, sweetheart, how are you?"

"I'm fine, mom." I love my mother dearly, but she's been a bit overbearing these past couple days, calling me every two hours since Greg took the last of his things out of the house. I sit at the table in the middle of the breakroom.

"Are you sure you don't want dad and I to come up there to spend some time with you?"

"Mom, you and dad knew Greg and I were getting a divorce months ago. He just took the last of his things out of the house two days ago. I'm fine. I'm happy he's gone."

I really am. "I need alone time anyway for self-reflection, healing and to make plans to sell the house. That *man* sent me an email yesterday that I have a month to get the house ready for sale."

Spiteful donkey hole. I hadn't planned to stay in the house anyway. Too many bad memories. I need a fresh start in every area of my life.

Mom grumbles under her breath. "Greg is the complete scum of the earth. The way he's been treating you is despicable. Let him conceive five babies and have to experience the horrible pain of losing them all..."

My eyes squeeze tight, suppressing the tears from the memories of what my body went through during each miscarriage. Greg was supportive and sensitive to my needs during the first two. The miscarriages that followed, he treated me like an infectious disease woman. Like an incomplete woman. Like I purposely lost each of our children.

It's a wonder I got pregnant so many times. The last time, while I laid on the cold, tile floor of our bathroom sobbing, with blood soaking my thighs, Greg walked in with disgust on his face.

"Get up so I can take your worthless body to the hospital." He walked out without helping me up from the floor. I knew then for sure I could no longer

be his wife and I could never put my body through that strain ever again.

"...Every dog will have their day. He will reap what he's sown." I listen to my mother while brushing aside the bad memories of Greg.

"For now, mom, I'm okay. I just started working at this pharmacy seven months ago, but after I move out of the house, I'm going to put in for a week off so I can come to South Carolina to visit with you and dad."

"Perfect! You are due some time away. Myrtle Beach would be the right antidote."

I smile. "It will be. Actually, I'll put in my request for time off tomorrow. We've only lived in the house for four years so there's not much to clear out. I should be out in a month like that *man* emphasized."

"Okay. I know Ray will be excited to have his baby girl come for a visit. Keep us posted on the move and when you're coming down here."

"I will." I look at the time on my wristwatch. "I have to get back to work. I'll call you tomorrow. Love you."

"Love you too, sweetie."

I am happy to be free of Greg, but I now feel lost. Lost on what to make of my life. I wasted so much time with him.

5

MALIK

The day after the job lead from Pharmacist Rae, I went to Judea's Bakery. Judea signed a contract with me to power wash the sidewalk of her business monthly and to bi-weekly take care of the lawn. Her bakery is in an older house that was rezoned for commercial property. She remodeled the house and turned it into an eat-in bakery and coffee shop. It's a nice, colonial-style house with an acre of lawn, with a full-grown Cherry Blossom tree out front, and two more out back. I can't wait to see them bloom next month in April. This contract has secured me an additional $650 a month.

Things are looking up.

I stopped by the pharmacy after my meeting with Judea so I could thank Rae again for her job lead, but she wasn't on shift. It's probably a good thing because I was feeling exuberant that day and might have asked her out on a date. I don't want her to be my rebound though. Again, for reasons beyond my understanding regarding Rae, when I do approach her in that way, I want all my ducks in order. There's something about *her* that intrigues me more than any woman has before.

Sitting on the edge of the bed in Drew's guest bedroom, I button up my long-sleeved shirt. I already have on dark chino pants and loafers. Though Drew's church has a casual vibe, I don't want to wear jeans and Timberlands.

There's a knock on the closed bedroom door. "You riding with us?" Drew asks.

"No, I'll meet you guys there." I stand to tuck my shirt in my pants.

"All right. We'll save you a seat."

"Thanks!"

***

I feel excitement building inside me the moment I step into the foyer of Journey to Faith Church in Alexandria, Virginia. It has me wondering why it's been nine years since I've graced a church with my presence. The last time was for my parent's funeral. There's no particular reason either. I'm a true bedside church service Christian. I listen to the Word every Sunday without fail on my phone or television, but I hadn't been inclined to attend a church since recently.

"Good morning, welcome to Journey to Faith. Are you a new visitor?" A white gentleman that looks to be in his late sixties greets me. He offers his hand and I accept it for a handshake.

"Good morning, Sir. Yes, I'm a visitor. My brother and his family attend here."

"Good. What's your brother's name?"

"Drew Day."

He looks like he's mentally going through a Rolodex in his mind. I'll be surprised if he knows them. This is a mega church – at least three thousand people attend.

"Yes, I know Drew and his wife, Deidre and son, Kason. They're a lovely family. I believe Deidre helps out in children's church and I know Drew and Kason attend Men's Bible study every other Saturday."

Wow.

Drew had invited me a few times to the Men's Bible study, but it's on Saturday mornings and I'm usually working.

"That's them. I'm amazed that you know who they are. You must greet thousands of people every Sunday."

He chuckles. "I may be getting older, but I still have a sharp mind and good memory."

"I hope to say the same in a few years."

"I'm sure you will. My name is Williams, what's yours?"

"Malik."

"It's a pleasure to meet you, son. I hope you enjoy service. It's about to begin and please don't let this be the last time I see you here."

"I have a feeling I'll be back."

I leave the nice man to continue greeting church attendees at the doors. I make my way through the sea of people towards the left-side sanctuary doors. Drew texted that they're saving a seat for me on that side.

Just as I walk into the massive sanctuary, the choir starts assembling on the stage. I'm directed by an usher to where Drew and Deidre are sitting in the middle row, end seats. Perfect. I prefer not to have to sit in the balcony.

"It's almost weird seeing you not wearing your grass-stained jeans and Timbs," Drew says after giving me a bro hug.

I got in late last night after shooting some pool with my boy, Saint. His name is so ironic because there's hardly anything saintly about him. But we've been friends since tenth grade, and other than my brother, I know he's got my back.

"I'm trying to be like you, Big Bro."

Drew is dressed almost identical to me expect his shirt is gray and mine is blue and he has on oxford shoes, whereas I'm wearing loafers.

"Y'all can definitely pass for twins." Deidre says after giving me a hug.

"Good morning, Journey to Faith Church! It's time for praise and worship," the worship leader speaks into the microphone.

The music begins...

"You know my name..." The first words to Tasha Cobbs' song, "You Know My Name" send chills up my spine. I instantly feel the presence of God. An awareness of Him like never before causes moisture to pool in my eyes.

What is this?

I haven't shed a tear since the death of my parents. Here I am in church, nine years since their funeral and I can't fight the tears. And church *just* started. With each word of the song, my soul is being ripped bare. God knows my name. My pain. My shame. My fear. My heart's desire.

"Oh, how you walk with me..." I sing along offkey, with my hands raised in praise. So, this is what I've been missing being a bedside Baptist. The energy of the congregation. The live singing and music. Being surrounded by other believers.

I can feel Drew and Deirdre's eyes on me, watching me openly praise God. I have never done this so boldly before; I can't help it. I feel arms wrap around me. Arms that can't be seen. I begin to sob. *Is this what it feels like being filled with the Spirit?*

"Jesussssss!" I shout.

"Let it out Malik, praise Him," Deidre coaxes from my side. "God's been waiting on you to get here."

"Oh, how you tell me, that I am your own..." I continue to sing.

RAE

"You know my name..." This song gets me every single time. Every. Single. Time. As an usher, I'm standing at the right-side sanctuary doors of Journey to Faith church, I lift my hand in praise.

Another reason I love working for a black-owned, neighborhood pharmacy is that I get Sundays off because the pharmacy is closed. I love my church. I am happy that after trying to persuade Greg to attend church with me over the years, he always refused, because with us getting a divorce, I would have hated possibly having to find another church if he decided to keep membership here. I have been a member at Journey to Faith church for four years and have been volunteering as an usher since.

I always feel God's presence here. Today, it feels even more prevalent. It could be because I've been on my knees praying daily for God to reveal His purpose for my life. The direction He wants me to take. And I have been releasing my burdens at His feet.

"Come to me, all you who are weary and burdened, and I will give you rest." Matthew 11:28 has been my devotional Scripture this past week. I no longer want to carry the weight of it all. I fully surrender to Him. This new chapter in my life is dedicated to Jehovah. I no longer want to rely on my own understanding.

MALIK

I left church feeling like a brand-new man. I have never had that experience after my weekly, at-home church services. There's definitely something positive about being in the house of the Lord. I signed up for church membership today and will make it a point to attend weekly and as often as possible. I will also be more aware of my Saturday work scheduling so I can fit in Men's Bible study whenever I can.

Drew, Deidre and Kason invited me to brunch with them and a few of their church buddies, but I declined. I want to get home to go over my notes from service and read over the Scriptures again that Pastor Michael had referenced. I'm serious about taking my faith in God to a deeper level.

I make a left onto Drew's street. Seconds later, the three-level, 2500 square-foot home comes into view. Along with the sight of Janae's car parked in the driveway.

"Man, not today." I have a good mind to drive right past the house, but if I don't deal with her now, she'll only come back and I don't want Drew and his family to deal with her drama.

I park next to her car and reluctantly get out of my truck. Janae exits her vehicle as well. She has on dark, skinny jeans and a designer hoodie since it's a chilly day in March.

"Why are you here, Janae?"

"Why am I here? You blocked me and you're asking why am I here?"

I stare blankly at her, not giving a verbal response. She is a 36-year-old, grown woman and acts like a juvenile.

"You're just going to stand there looking dumb, Malik? It's been four days and you haven't come home."

I'm starting to think I missed the signs of her being bipolar. I sigh deeply.

"Janae, four days ago you kicked me out of my apartment. You pretty much told me our relationship is over – that you want nothing to do with me. I agreed. I left. I'm not coming back. We are done! My lease is up in about two weeks, so you'll have to find another place to live, or renew the lease on your own. Don't try to contact me anymore. And do not show up here at my brother's house again." I move to walk away.

"It's like that, Malik? We have been together for four years and you're walking away this easily?"

I turn around to face her. "Why do you want to be with a man that ain't shit?" I throw her words back at her. She already has me backsliding in my renewed faith. Even more reason for us not to be together.

Her face scrunches up, then she sucks her teeth. "How am I supposed to pay the rent by myself?"

"You make 60K a year, right? You've made it a point to bring that up every chance you got. My lil' 35K is chump change since I don't make the big bucks anymore. I think you can handle the rent and everything else just fine."

She laughs bitterly. "This is exactly why I put you out. Only a worthless man doesn't make sure his woman is taken care of."

Yet she's still living in my apartment.

"You are not my woman. And when you were, you were too ungrateful to realize I did everything to make sure you didn't have to spend a dime of your money if you didn't want to. All the best finding the next man that would put up with your selfishness. Now get in your car and leave my brother's property."

"Trust me, the next man will be way better than you. I don't even know why I came here. I had a moment of insanity, feeling sorry for you being homeless and broke. What grown man lives with his brother and his family? You're pathetic!" Janae sashays to her car and gets in. I watch her reverse, then drive away.

6

RAE

"No, Mrs. Ward, you must eat something first before you take your medication, or you will have an upset stomach." I speak to the eighty-year-old woman on the phone. "Yes. And make sure you follow up with your doctor when you've finished all the pills...You're welcome. Goodbye." I hang up the phone at my station in the pharmacy.

"She was gagging again?" Yasmine asks from her position across from me. She's bagging a filled prescription then scanning and putting a label on the bag.

"Yup. I told her yesterday when she got the medicine to eat something first. It doesn't help that she hates taking pills, but that medicine isn't available in liquid form."

"At least she only has to take it for six more days."

"Hmmm." I busy myself with all things … meds. I check to make sure the prescription in the bin in front of me is the correct dosage and won't cause any drug interactions with other meds, or an allergic reaction in the patient.

"Have you heard Chris Brown is coming to DC for a concert? You and I should go together. Now that you're single, you need to let loose and have some fun. I know you're almost forty, but you and I look the same age. You might snag a lil' Tenderoni."

It's a little after nine in the morning, so the store is quiet right now. Most people come in right before noon to place or pick up their prescriptions.

I laugh at her mention of a Tenderoni. "There are a few songs of his I've heard on the radio that I like, but I don't know about going to a concert."

"It'll be fun…"

The hairs on the back of my neck stand at attention. My spine goes ramrod straight. I tilt my head to the left. Greg is approaching the pharmacy counter with a scowl on his once handsome face. Admittedly, he's still physically a good-looking man. His nasty behavior towards me makes him hideous.

Yasmine noticed him first and stopped what she's doing to greet him at the counter. "Good morning, are you here to drop off or pick up a prescription?" She's so good at what she does, but Greg doesn't deserve her friendly customer service.

Greg ignores Yasmine and shoots daggers my way. "I need to have a word with you." He doesn't ask; he tells me. It is almost unbelievable to know that this man used to love me once. Once upon a time…no fairytale ending.

I grit my teeth to stop myself from cussing him out. The audacity of this man showing up on my job is madness. I push away from the workstation. "Yasmine, I'll be right back."

"You sure? I can call Paul." Paul is the security guard on duty today. I like that Yasmine can pick up on Greg's visit being unwelcomed. I'm not afraid of him though. He had become verbally abusive, but he wasn't stupid enough to lay a finger on me. My dad made sure I knew self-defense since I was his only daughter and child. I take self-defense classes regularly to keep my skills.

"Yeah, I'm good. We'll be in the breakroom," I tell her. I look at Greg. "Meet me by that door." I point out for him the door that reads *Employees Only*.

I open the door for Greg and he silently follows me to the breakroom. It gives me seconds to get my mind right when it comes to dealing with him.

"Why are you here?" I ask, turning to face him. I stand leaning against the counter.

"You're not returning any of my calls." He stands in the doorway.

"You have no reason to call me. Anything you need me to know, you can tell my lawyer and she'll relay the message to me."

His jaw ticks. "You're not getting seventy percent of the proceeds from the house when it's sold."

"Yes, I am."

"The hell you are. It's fair that we both get fifty."

I want to laugh. He's talking about being fair? Really Greg?

"What's fair is that I put down two hundred thousand for the down payment. Both of us contributed to the mortgage which means I should get the greater portion of the proceeds." Even though I took breaks in working during the pregnancies, when I did work, I made much more than he did. And I had been building a nest egg since my parents had given me fifty thousand dollars after they sold their house in North Carolina before moving to Myrtle Beach.

"You definitely are a bitter, barren bitch. I'm glad once the house is sold, I won't have to deal with you again."

"And I'm glad I no longer have the agony of calling you my husband." I smile brightly. "Have a nice day, Greg." Killing him with kindness. He hates it when his digs at me doesn't render the reaction he wants.

Succumbing to the fact that he will be wasting his breath having a verbal battle with me, Greg turns and leaves. I don't move until I hear the *Employee's Only* door close shut.

Back in my position at the pharmacy counter, I use work to keep my mind off my unpleasant visitor.

"Rae, so check this. I'm throwing you a divorce party. Because if you were married to him for six years, you deserve a celebration for no longer being his wife."

"A divorce party?" I go back to my workstation to finish what I was doing before Greg's unpleasant visit.

"Yup. We're both working the morning shift on Saturday, so I'm taking you out that night."

Working with Yasmine is cool, but I don't know about hanging out together outside of work. Also, I'm a homebody. Outside of my new condo I leased a couple weeks ago, the only places I frequent are work and church...

"No ma'am! Get outside your head now. I know your hermit self, trying to talk yourself out of it. You are young and single and we're going to mingle. That butthole ex of yours is not going to rob you of your joy any longer. And I know you uphold Christian values, but God has no problem with you having good, clean fun."

I smile because it's nice having someone other than my parents champion me. I need a friend like her. Inside and outside of work.

"Okay. We can celebrate my divorce."

"Yes! And I'm going to hook you up with an outfit."

I raise my brow curiously.

Yasmine waves me off. "Trust me. I won't do you wrong."

"Fine! But you better make sure I don't regret this."

Yasmine starts dancing where she stands, bagging filled prescriptions. "Saturday is gonna be lit!"

***

I look at myself in the full-length mirror in my bedroom. I look amazing. Yasmine bought me a royal blue, halter skater dress that falls right above my knees. I paired it with nude, strap heels. My hair is styled in a twist out. I'm wearing my signature, large hoop, gold earrings and gold cuff bracelet. I kept my makeup simple, only enhancing my brows and lashes, and I have bold red lips.

"If I played for the other team, we wouldn't be leaving here tonight." Yasmine comes into view behind me in the mirror. "You don't look good. You look goodt!" She sings the letter "T."

"Thanks to you. This dress fits me perfectly."

"It does. Told you I would hook you up. You deserve this. I don't know your full story, but the brief encounter I had with Greg told me you need a Rae Day....well Rae Night. And tonight, we're going dancing, karaoke and maybe even to shoot some pool. The Spot near the National Harbor is where we can do all of that."

I have to admit, I'm looking forward to having fun tonight. It's been a long time since I just kicked back and relaxed. Breathed. I need this.

The Spot is essentially *the spot* to be at on a Saturday night. I have heard of it before, but this is my first time here. Yasmine and I are lucky to make it in before they reach the 300-capacity limit. There are three main sections. The lounge area where there's a stage and seating with tables. Game area where there's four pool tables surrounded by players and spectators. People are at tables playing dominoes and card games, and you can shoot darts. The third section is the bar area with additional seating and tables.

Yasmine and I make our way to the lounge area, not without appreciative glances from men. If I look "goodt," Yasmine is smoking hot in her silver strapless jumpsuit. She is the embodiment of a young twenty-something. We both wore light jackets since it's still chilly in April, but we took them off the moment we walked in.

"Here's to being free of Greg!" Yasmine and I clink our shot glasses together, then drink. We've been at The Spot for less than an hour, enjoying the brave souls to grace the small stage for karaoke. After eating a basket of French fries and calamari, Yasmine persuades me to do tequila shots. I committed to one, but the burn down my throat is so good, I want another. That's my limit.

"To starting over!" I pick up my second shot glass clink it with hers. "Thank you for bringing me out tonight."

Yasmine looks at me from across the tiny, round table. "You're welcome. But the night just got started." She starts gyrating in her seat when the beat for "Lights, Camera, Action" by Mr. Cheeks drops. My hips inadvertently start moving. This used to be my jam.

"Let's dance!" Yasmine pulls my arm, taking me to the dance floor with her.

I hesitate when we hit the floor. "I'm not a good public dancer."

Yasmine shakes her head at me and says, over the music, "I believe every woman should be ratchet at least once in her life and I have a feeling you ain't never did. Squat low and pop that booty." Yasmine demonstrates for me.

What the heck. I came here to let loose and have fun celebrating my divorce so that's what I do. I stop thinking and begin feeling...feeling the beat and letting it lead the way. I squat as low as my almost forty-year-old knees will allow and attempt to pop my booty. I laugh, feeling the exhilaration of the moment. I get in a groove.

"Okay, girl. I'm now starting to think you have done this before. Get it, get it." Yasmine cheers me on while dancing beside me.

Moments later I feel butterflies flutter in my belly. The last time that happened, it was because of *him*. That dark-skinned brotha that came to pick up a prescription at the pharmacy too many weeks ago. Could it be him standing behind me? I freeze in place on the dance floor. An arm encircles my waist.

"Pharmacist Rae Cooper." My name sounds perfect from his lips. "I'm really happy God blessed me with your essence tonight." His other hand goes to my waist and I turn in his arms.

I look up. This man is too gorgeous for his own good. "What's your name?" I ask desperate to know before I do something stupid like tug on his full beard to bring his lips closer and kiss him.

The music transitions to "Pole Dancer" by Wale featuring Megan Thee Stallion.

He flashes me a smile that sends a signal to every erogenous zone in my body. "Malik Day. Can I have this dance? Though I'm not much of a dancer, but I can be your pole to lean on."

Oh Gawd. I'm going to have to repent for all the thoughts running through my mind right now. I bite down on my bottom lip while nodding my head. I start dancing again, turning so my back is to him. Yasmine gives me an approving wink. She's killing it with her dance moves. I play it safe dancing without my back touching his front. I don't need the temptation. Malik's hands find my waist again, but he doesn't tug me closer, respecting the invisible line I created. We silently dance to the song. More so me than him. This night is already memorable, and it hasn't even ended.

When the song is almost over, Malik leans closer, his beard tickles my cheek. "I just got out of a four-year, toxic relationship and I have some personal things I need to work on, but I promise you when I get myself together to approach you correctly, I'm coming to find you." Malik kisses me on the side of my neck, causing my heart to skip a beat. He steps away from me and I miss him instantly. "Be expecting me to come for you."

I turn to watch him walk away leaving me heartbroken, relieved, and turned on. I hope *I'm* ready when he comes back.

7

MALIK

It's been six months since my life changed for the better. Janae is long gone, my faith in God is stronger than ever, and business is picking up. My connect with Judea's Bakery helped me secure a contract with her brother, Judah, who owns a shopping complex in La Plata, Maryland. He hired my company to take care of the biweekly pressure washing of 300 feet of sidewalks.

Then their baby sister, Jada, hired my company to take care of the landscaping at her bed and breakfast in Washington, DC. Based on my financial projections, I may gross close to $90,000 this year. Next year, for sure, will be even better. I had to hire my boy, Saint, on a part-time basis to help me out.

"See now, had you called first, there wouldn't have been a problem. You walked in on something that could have been avoided had you given me heads up that you were coming to my house." Saint talks loudly on his Bluetooth to one of the three women he deals with while straightening out the water hoses for me to power the sidewalk.

He's a well-paid barber, but helps me out three days a week around his schedule. Saint keeps me, Drew and Kason's fades tight. He also maintains his own head full of shoulder-length dreads, which he has pulled back into a ponytail today.

I don't know how he does it. Some men, like me, only want to be in a relationship with *one* woman. My dad would roll over in his grave if I were to disrespect a woman. He taught Drew and I how to love, care and respect the woman we commit ourselves to. I have never cheated in any of my relationships. When I commit myself to a woman, she's my only focus and I expect the same from her.

Saint though? He will probably break out in hives if he doesn't have at least two women in his life. Here's the thing though – he's always up front with the women he deals with. They know from the jump he is not a one-woman man. Yet they agree, then can't deal with what they agreed to. Hence Saint's current conversation.

"...You ain't the only one and will never be, Kita. You knew this from the start so I'm not arguing with you about what you saw last night. Wait for me to meet up with you later and we continue what we got, or we can end this now...Okay cool. It's been good knowing you for three months." Saint ends the call.

I shake my head at him. "See, that's why I can only be with one woman. Juggling three has to be a headache."

"It's only a headache when a chick doesn't play by the rules." He walks over to the diesel pressure washer next to my pickup truck. "But when are you hooking up with someone? It's been six months since Janae, and other than that woman you were dancing with months back at The Spot, you've been solo. Do I need to be worried?" He gives me a serious look.

I laugh while shaking my head. "Bruh, don't play. After dealing with Janae, I needed a break from being in a relationship to get my head straight and my business back on top. And that woman you remember me dancing with, I'm getting myself ready to approach her with my shi – my life in order." I stop myself from cussing. I didn't curse much before, but now I'm more conscious of it. I'm serious about living a godlier life. Some days are easier than others.

"Man, what you need to do is give yourself a year to run through some hoes. You've been a one-woman man since high school days."

"That ain't me. I like keeping the windows in my truck."

"That happened to me one time. And that's why I'm up front with these women so they have no reason to be salty."

"Man, whatever. You need to come to church with me on Sunday."

"I said I would. I do need a Christian woman on my roster," he says rubbing his chin.

Help him, Lord.

"Start the machine." I hold the handle for the surface cleaner and start hot-water pressure washing the sidewalk of the shopping center. The businesses on this side have less foot traffic which makes it easier to work during early evening hours. We have caution cones situated blocking off each section as we work.

Minutes later, I turn off the surface cleaner when I notice two women walking towards us. One of which looks annoyingly familiar in blue scrubs.

"Well looka here. My broke homeless Ex." Janae stops in front of me. Her friend snickers at her remark.

"And you're the gold-digger that robbed his pocket," Saint snarls at Janae. He never liked her. The saying, "love is blind," is true because it seems everyone in my life caught on to Janae's scheme faster than I did.

Janae shoots daggers at Saint and he mean mugs her back.

I inspect the sidewalk area that I just finished cleaning to make sure I got all the gum and stains up. "I'm not too broke for you to keep calling my phone from random numbers. Keep it up and I'll have to sic Deidre on you."

"Please, I have better things to do than call your phone," Janae tries to deflect, probably not expecting me to call her out in front of her friend.

I lift my head to look over at her. "You want me to play your voice message from yesterday?"

Her friend gives her a skeptical look.

"I have work to do, Janae. Be on your way so we can finish." Trying to be the bigger person with her is an exhausting job.

"Gladly." Janae starts to walk away then drops her large cup of smoothie on the freshly power washed sidewalk creating an orange mess. "Oops. Looks like you missed a spot."

Her friend gives her an annoyed look. I can see who's the mature one. "Girl, you're petty. Let these hardworking men do their jobs." She walks away with Janae following behind.

"Bruh, I know you don't like calling women outside their name, but she's a pure breed, female dog. Thank God you got out of that without any kids. Can you imagine her being your kids' mother?"

The thought makes me cringe.

8

RAE

Today is one of those days I want to crawl under a rock and die. September 23rd. My first miscarriage. Noah was the name I gave him. Though I lost the baby at ten weeks with no clue of the sex, I just know in my heart he was a boy. Greg thought I was insane naming all our fetuses. It helped me to cope and to properly grieve the loss of my babies.

Noah would have been five…

I have the day off. I requested it because I believed I wouldn't be able to handle smiling and greeting customers at the pharmacy counter for eight hours. Now I'm regretting the decision. Work may have been more beneficial than lying in bed staring at the walls with my mind in overdrive, going over the "should-haves" that could have prevented my miscarriages.

I should have taken better vitamins. I should have had healthier eating habits. I should have never stood in front of the microwave as a kid…

I throw the covers off me and get out of bed. *I will not stay cooped up inside all day. This is the day the Lord has made, and I will rejoice in it.*

Father God, help me.

I push the tears from my eyes while heading to the adjoined bathroom. I hate days like these because no matter how hard I try to *not* be depressed, the effort makes me feel even more worthless, if that makes sense.

Twenty minutes later, after a quick shower, dressing in black joggers and a plain white t-shirt and brushing my hair back in a low afro-puff ponytail, I make my way out of the house. It takes me less than fifteen minutes to get to Judea's Bakery. This place has the best coffee and baked goods. They rival Starbucks, in my opinion.

I arrive at the perfect time. The morning rush is gone and there's only a few patrons sitting at tables enjoying their fresh pastry and drinks. I order a large espresso and a blueberry muffin. I find a table to sit at off to the side. The first sip of coffee and the aroma sets my mind at ease.

"The righteous cry out, and the Lord hears them; He delivers them from all their troubles." Psalm 34:17.

Some people are skeptical about the Christian faith. Faith in a God that isn't seen – to them at least. I see God all around me. I feel Him too. Like right now, I see Him in the little boy sitting next to a woman I assume is his mom. The little, redhead boy's infectious laugh brings a smile to my face. My heart is still heavy, however, instances like this assure me that God hears my cries.

I'm not as bad today as I was years ago –
months ago even. For that I'm thankful. There was a
time when seeing mothers with their young children
gutted me. I'm healing. One day, this *day* won't hurt
anymore.

"Pharmacist Rae Cooper." Butterflies flutter in
my belly at the baritone voice.

"Malik Day," I say when he comes into view,
sitting in the seat in front of me. I have a cheesy grin
on my face, despite my depressed mood.

Malik smiles back at me, killing me softly. "You
remembered my name."

"You're a hard man to forget," I respond
truthfully. The memory of us on the dance floor has
played in a loop in my mind for months. Who could
forget this dark chocolate perfection of a man?
Certainly not me.

"That's good to know." He unabashedly lets his eyes roam over my face. Now I'm regretting not putting much effort into my appearance.

Pushing my vanity aside, I also take the opportunity to visually drink him in. My fingers itch to stroke his full, dark beard. His dark brown eyes speak of promises I'm anxious to know if he will keep. Malik is dressed similar to the first time I met him – a plain t-shirt, jeans and Timberland boots. It's such an ordinary attire that he makes look sexy as sin.

"I notice the lawn outside looks impeccable. You have anything to do with that?" I pick up my cup to take a sip of coffee.

"I never did properly thank you for this job lead." He nods his head. "Thank you!"

"You're welcome," I smile. He stares at me so intently I can hardly breathe. "What?" I self consciously pull at my afro-puff.

"Something tells me…" He places his forearms on the table leaning forward, looking me in my eyes. "…You need me today."

Those darn butterflies in my belly again. "I need *you*?"

"I know I'm still a stranger to you, so you don't have to tell me what's wrong right now. But…please let me take you out on a date. I want to spend the rest of the day keeping a smile on your face."

Yes, please!

"How do you know I don't have a significant other?" I play coy because, like he said, we're strangers. I'm also not ready to examine the complete ease I feel around him and the comfort of knowing that if he asks, I would easily tell him why this day is usually hard for me.

Talking about my miscarriages isn't something I willingly divulge, not even with my closest friends. My new friend, Yasmine, doesn't even know all the details. But *him*. He makes me feel I won't be considered a freak in his eyes.

"Do you?" The look on his face tells me he already knows the answer to his question.

I shake my head. "No, but –"

"I give you my word I'm not a criminal. I'll bring you back in one piece. You can even tell Judea you're riding with me and leaving your car here. That way someone knows what name to give the police if something happens – which it won't." He flashes a smile.

How can I say no?

"Okay. But I should probably go home and change."

"You are perfect. You don't need to change."

I blush behind my cup of coffee. It's been *too* long since a man inadvertently told me I'm beautiful – at least that's my interpretation of what he said.

"I had a residential job scheduled and was on my way when the customer called to reschedule. I'm all yours for the day."

What about tomorrow? I don't ask that out loud though. I'm not ready for the answer. Quite frankly, I'm not sure I'm ready for more than today.

"All right, Malik Day, what's on your agenda for keeping a smile on my face?"

After a quick stop at Walmart, Malik takes me to a park...with swings and slides and monkey bars, and pedal boating and a fishing pier and picnic pavilions.

"A park?" I state the obvious when he parks his truck in the lot at Gilbert Run Park.

"Yup. Sometimes as adults, I think we take ourselves too seriously. Remember as a kid, when your only concern was which cartoon you were going to watch on a Saturday morning? Or skipping a bar on the monkey bars? Or winning a game of marbles?"

I smile at the thought. Life really was so much easier then. Now look at us as adults – stressed with too many responsibilities.

"How old are you?" His mention of playing marbles has me guessing he's around my age, though he looks younger. And well...it would be nice to know the age of the man I'm spending the day with. I hope he isn't that much younger than me. I'd hate to see the disappointed look on his face when I tell him I'm forty.

Why should it matter when you're only spending today together?

"Thirty-seven. How old are you?"

"Forty. Today's my birthday."

Malik's eyes widen in surprise. "You should have said something sooner. I would have gotten cupcakes to go with our lunch later. Happy fortieth birthday, Rae. I'm happy you agreed to spend your birthday with me."

His perfect smile is one of the best gifts I've ever received...he has already taken my mind off the other reason this day has been hard on me.

"Thank you! Your quick trip in Walmart included getting lunch?"

He had insisted I stay in the truck while he ran into the store. He wanted to keep things a surprise. I did notice he had bought a small cooler.

"Mmm hmm." He reaches for the door handle. "Stay put. I'm going around to open your door for you." I watch him get out of the truck and walk around to my side, opening the door for me. "How about we hit the playground first?" he asks after helping me out of the truck.

The weather today is perfect to be outdoors. Seventy-eight degrees, not extremely hot with a hint of breeze.

"Sure." I feel myself getting excited. I probably haven't been to a playground since...actually I have no clue as to the last time I've been on a playground.

Malik takes my hand in his, leading the way. The move is so natural. His calloused hands in mine feels meant to be. This man is a stranger though. No matter how nice he has been now and in all our previous encounters, I know hardly anything about him, and him me. With that thought, I remind myself that, just for today, he's the friend I need. Nothing more.

Malik gives my hand a gentle squeeze. "Sit, I'll push you."

I give him a skeptical look as we stand in front of the swings. There are two women here watching three kids play on the playground. I begin to feel self-conscious and absolutely ridiculous about the thought of sitting on a children's swing.

"Stop thinking and just do it. See those kids over there?" He gestures to the trio laughing as they take turns on the slide. "They couldn't care less that we're over here. They are having the time of their little lives just going down a slide. They have no worries because they know their mom will take care of any dangers or concerns. God wants you to not have any worries either, Rae. Today is your birthday, but something tells me that sad look I see in your eyes, despite your best efforts to hide it, isn't because today is the day you were born. There's something more. God wants you to be like those kids."

I watch the two little girls and boy…God, I want that carefree joy. That unexplainable peace.

"Let me push you on the swing." Malik pulls me from my thoughts.

I let go of his hand and go over to sit on the swing. "I would rather you get on the swing next to me and we see who can go the highest."

"You ain't said nothing but a word." Malik cockily walks over to the swing to my left. "This was my thang when I was eight." He laughs and I join in with him.

"Ha! We'll see. I was the best at this in Mrs. Clark's third grade class," I brag. I begin moving on the swing, pumping my much bigger legs to go higher than my eight-year-old self ever could.

I look over at Malik. His big, manly body looks so comical swinging back and forth. And it causes my heart to bloom with affection.

I need to be careful with him. He can cause me fall for him too easily. A man like him deserves a woman who can give him little miniature versions of himself. But, I'm not that woman. Never will be.

"You're losing steam there, Rae," Malik calls out.

Malik is swinging way too high in the air. As a kid going that high was fun. Now I'm all too aware of the dangers my five foot five, one-hundred- and fifty-five-pound self can encounter if I fall.

"Because I'm much bigger now than I was then and I'm not in the mood for busting my head today." I laugh while still swinging blissfully back and forth.

Malik slows to my safe pace. "You're right. I don't want anything bruising your beautiful face."

"You are charming."

And refreshing. And apparently you have a relationship with God that I find endearing. And you don't remind me of Greg.

"Thank you, my charm has a lot to do with the beautiful woman before me. Also, my parents taught me well."

I blush. "Please thank them for me."

Malik turns away from me, looking ahead. "I believe they heard you. They were killed in a boating accident nine years ago."

The revelation leaves me momentarily speechless. At forty, I'm not ready to imagine the world without my parents, so I can only imagine the pain he still feels years later. "I'm sorry for your loss…Do you have any siblings?"

"Thanks. Yes, I have an older brother. How about you?"

"I'm my parents' only child."

"Oh man, don't tell me you were one of those spoiled kids that didn't want anyone playing with their toys."

I laugh out loud because he read me well. Sobering up, I reply, "Yes. I was that kid until I got a rude awakening in kindergarten when Timothy Morley pushed my stacked building blocks down during playtime. I was being a meanie, hogging all the blocks from everyone. He pushed down my version of a castle I built and told me, 'If you won't share with anyone no one will ever be your friend again.'

"Then he and the other kids stuck their tongues out at me before walking away. Of course, me being the center of my own world, didn't take his threat seriously until a week later, none of my classmates would play with me. That's when I begged my mom to bake cupcakes for my class. I brought the cupcakes to school and asked my teacher if I could address the class. I apologized for being mean and asked them to be my friends again. They all forgave me and during lunch I passed out cupcakes to everyone."

"I would have wanted two cupcakes before I forgave you," Malik teases.

I surprise myself by flirting back. "And I would have given you two."

Malik watches me swinging back and forth and I can tell by the look in his eyes that he wants to reply to what I said, but instead he says, "The kids are gone, Let's go down the slide." He jumps off the swing.

I smile. "You must come here often with your kids." It is my not so low-key way of finding out if he has children.

"I don't have any children. But I used to bring my nephew, Kason, here a lot when he was younger. Come, I'll push you down."

I follow him to the double slides. We have to climb up a few steps to get to the top. The playground equipment is big and sturdy enough to accommodate adults as well as children.

Malik stands before the red slide and I go to the yellow.

"Wanna race?" I ask, putting aside the fact that we are two grown adults playing like little children. This is the most carefree I've been since that night months ago when we danced together. I *need* more moments like this.

I position myself at the top of the slide, grateful it can easily accommodate my size eight frame.

"Yes, winner gets to pick the movie we're going to see later."

"Okay!" I exclaim, excited more by the fact that I'll be spending even more time with him later. If this is the only day, I'll allow myself with him, I may as well get as much time in as possible.

"You cheated!"

Malik beats me down by three seconds. I'm laughing, running back to get up the steps to the slides. "We're doing it again."

He chuckles and it's now my new favorite sound. "I'll allow you a head start." He leisurely climbs the steps behind me.

"Nope! I'm winning fair and square."

Malik beats me down the slide again, and again, and again – I'm having the time of my life on a freaking playground on my fortieth birthday.

I could never have imagined this.

I guess I did need *him* today.

In my distress I called upon the Lord; to my God I cried for help. From his temple he heard my voice, and my cry to him reached his ears. Psalm 18:6

Thank you, God, for hearing my cries for help.

"Are you hungry? I can start the grill for lunch."

He must have heard my stomach growling. It's after 12pm and I only had a cup of coffee and half a muffin for breakfast.

"You bought food to grill?"

"Yes." He takes my hand in his and we walk back to the truck.

I never thought of the perfect date. Not that this is one, but if I had ever thought of a perfect date – this would be at the top of the list. A day at the park, cooking on the grill.

I help Malik set up for lunch, taking the items out of the cooler he bought, and two filled grocery bags, placing them on the picnic table under the pavilion near the grill. We're the only ones here.

"I wasn't sure what you like to eat so I played it safe and got chicken to grill. But, if you're a vegetarian, I bought one of those prepackaged salads. One of the clerks told me they're pretty good."

I bite down on my lip to prevent the smile that threatens to blossom on my face. *Lord, why would you send this wonderful, thoughtful man into my life when I can't give him everything a whole woman can?*

I question myself. *Who says he wants anything more?*

I recall Malik's words a few months ago during our second encounter. *I just got out of a four year toxic relationship and I have some personal things I need to work on, but I promise you when I get myself together to approach you correctly, I'm coming to find you.*

But I have nothing to offer Malik – or any other man.

The Holy Spirit chastises me immediately. *Don't allow the enemy to trick you into thinking that your lack of birthing a child makes you less than a woman.* My harsh reality, however, makes it hard to receive at times.

I clear my head of my wayward thoughts. "I'm not a vegetarian, but I'll eat the salad along with the grilled chicken." I offer him a smile. "What can I do to help?"

9

MALIK

"Would you mind seasoning the chicken while I clean off the grill?" I had bought jugs of water, cleaning supplies, food seasoning, gloves, knives and more to get the job done. Now knowing that today is Rae's fortieth birthday, I would have preferred she just sit back and relax while I catered to her. But I have the feeling she needs the distraction of doing something helpful.

"Sure."

We work in companionable silence. I keep stealing glances at her, admiring how naturally beautiful she is. Her face is makeup free. Her natural hair is styled in a low afro puff ponytail that I'm curious to see let free from the hair tie. The jogger and t-shirt she has on accentuates her glorious curves. I may be more on the straight and narrow now in regards to my faith, but I'm still a man. Rae is definitely a woman. A whole lotta woman.

I want her to be mine.

From the day I met her, that thought has been blaring in my heart and mind. I keep wondering if it's the sign everyone gets when they find – *the one.*

I don't know.

What I do know is she's been on my mind for six months since I saw her behind the pharmacy counter. Five months ago, I saw her on the dance floor at The Spot and I had to approach her and stake my claim, in a sense, for the other dudes looking. I had to let her know I would be coming to find her once I got my life in order.

I hadn't exactly planned on that day being today. God, however, knows best. Because there's no way I'm letting her slip away.

"Okay, what do you call a pig that does karate?" I ask, before biting into my grilled corn on the cob.

Rae is sitting across from me at the picnic table. She's been tearing into her grilled chicken, corn on the cob and salad without an ounce of self-consciousness, enjoying her food. It's another thing I like about her. Some women tend to act shy eating in front of a man.

Rae covers her mouth with her hand, swallowing before answering. "I don't know." Her lip twitches with a smile, awaiting my reply.

All of the jokes I've been sharing with her are silly, but it's keeping a smile on her face. Which is my mission for the day. "A *pork chop*! Get it?"

Rae nods her head, laughing. "These jokes are so corny, but funny."

She's so easy to please. And it's refreshing.

"You think I should take my show on the road?"

"I think you should stick with rebuilding your business. I'm sure you'll have a crew of employees working full-time for you soon."

I had shared with Rae the struggles I have been dealing with in my business and that her job lead was the beginning of things moving in a better direction.

Her belief in me massages my ego, which endears her to me more.

One thing a man really wants from a woman is for her to believe in him. Believe in his talents and abilities. And hearing it from his woman is the biggest encouragement ever.

Rae isn't my woman – yet. Her words of encouragement mean nothing less, even though she isn't.

"Thank you. I guess I'll be keeping this a one-audience show." I wink at her. She blushes before picking up her lemonade.

"Why are frogs so happy?"

"Because they live doubles lives, in sea and on land?"

"Good one! But that's not my answer."

"What is it then?"

"They eat whatever *bugs* them."

She laughs. "I'm taking a wild guess – you were the class clown in school?"

"I wasn't. But my friend Saint was. You'll meet him soon." I throw that last part in there because I want her to know today isn't the last she'll see of me. "I was more of a prankster. I gave some of my teachers and classmates hell." I smile at the nostalgia. "I'm almost certain my future kids will be payback for my teen years."

I watch the smile dissolve from Rae's face.

Was it something I said?

With her head down, Rae begins picking through her salad with the fork.

"Do you have children?" I ask the simple question. Something in my gut though says it's more than that.

She stabs at the lettuce, tomatoes, and cucumbers a few times before replying. "Today is my birthday and..." She lifts her head to look at me. Tears are pooling in her eyes.

My heart constricts tightly at the hopeless look in her eyes and the anticipation of what will come out of her mouth next.

"...the fifth anniversary of my *first* miscarriage."

Oh!

"I've had five miscarriages in six years. Each time I hoped, I prayed, I begged God for that child to make it at least to the safe zone to be born prematurely. But they never did. My ex-husband, the man who promised to love me forever, became the enemy. I already felt worthless as a woman more and more after each miscarriage – he made me feel one hundred times worse. After the last one – I finally came to the realization I couldn't put my body through that strain and disappointment anymore. And I could no longer stay married to him.

"Days like today are still tough for me, though it's a whole lot better than before. And today..." She wipes the tears that fell from her eyes. "...has been one of the best birthdays I've had in years. Thank you!"

I want to pull her onto my lap and hold her tightly to my chest until all her pain and sadness dissipates.

And who the hell is that jerk she was married to?

"So, can you please continue telling me jokes? And there's an action comedy movie at the theatres I wouldn't mind seeing, even though you did beat me on the slide, *cheating*." Her lips twitch with a smile, despite the sad look in her eyes.

I desperately want to hold her and kiss and chase all her giants away. I follow her lead in not letting what she just revealed put a damper on our day. I find comfort in the fact that she trusted me with her truth.

"I won fair and square. But I'm down for the action comedy." I push my empty plate to the side on the picnic table. "What's the most famous creature in the ocean?"

Rae swallows her forkful of salad before answering. "I don't know."

"A *starfish*."

She almost chokes on a laugh. "Of course."

***

After lunch in the park, then riding on the paddle boat, Rae and I caught a 4:15pm show at AMC theatre. After the nearly two hours show, I took her to dinner at Red Lobster. She said she had a craving for their biscuits and All-You-Can-Eat shrimp.

I just parked my truck alongside Rae's SUV in the parking lot of Judea's Bakery. We're the only cars in the lot at 8:06pm. The Bakery and coffee shop closes at 6pm on weekdays.

I'm not ready for Rae to go.

She must know this if my driving less than 40 mph to get back here wasn't enough indication.

Rae shifts in her seat to face me with her back against the passenger door. "Malik, I can't thank you enough for today. I've enjoyed your company. I don't think I'll ever forget this day."

"Why does that sound like you won't be seeing me again?"

She finally addresses the elephant in the room...truck. "Well I...I remember what you said that night on the dance floor...about coming back for me when you got your life in order. But...Malik you deserve a woman who," She looks away from me.

I reach over and gently turn her face back towards me with my fingers on her cheek.

"I like you...a lot. In one day, I've seen what a wonderful man you are. A man that deserves a woman that can give you *everything* you want –"

"I don't care that you're not able to birth children, Rae. I get it. We're too old to beat around the bush about our desires, needs and expectations. So, let me clarify. I want you! I want to date you. And if God sees fit, I want you to one day be my wife. Do I want children? Yes. We can explore options on making that happen. But make no mistake, I want you, Rae. And I hope with everything in me you want me to." I lay my heart bear.

Risking it all.

Our day together strengthened my need for her in my life. I have prayed, *send her to me Lord*. I'm convinced she's my answered prayer.

"You want, *me*?"

I cup her face with my hands. Our faces are drawing nearer to each other. "Yes. Will you have me?"

"Yes," Rae replies, but it is hesitant. Tears pool in her eyes. "I'm scared, but I do want to give whatever this is between us a try." Rae brings her arms around my neck, pulling me further towards her lips.

She tastes like a hint of shrimp scampi, mints and pure perfection.

Rae moans against my mouth. I force myself to pull away from her delectable lips. The old me would've had her across the console and in my lap doing things I would have to pray for forgiveness for.

The new me is trying the Jesus thing the right way. Wait.

But she tastes too good.

Rae's chest rises and falls rapidly as she catches her breath. I look away from the lust in her eyes. I know she sees it reflected in mine too.

"There's something else you need to know if you want to date me," Rae breaks the silence in the truck. "To remain strong in my Christian faith, I'm practicing celibacy. This is new to me; I was married for six years and before that – I didn't think anything about sex before marriage. Now I do."

I turn to face her. Relieved that we're on the same page. The good Lord knows this celibacy practice will be hard for me too. If Rae wasn't game, I don't know how I would make it. It's been six months since I've had sex and today, this moment, makes it all the more real.

Lord, help me. Please!

"I rededicated my life to Christ and I'm practicing celibacy too."

Rae looks at me with awe. "You can't be real." She pokes me in the cheek with her slender finger. I pretend to bite at it when she pulls it away, which causes us both to laugh, and relieves some of the sexual tension.

"I'm real and I want us to explore dating the Christian way. We'll have to hold each other accountable to not break our vow of celibacy. You think we can handle it?"

Rae nods her ahead in agreement. "It will be tough..." She eyes me like I'm filet mignon and she's starved. "...but we can handle it. I hope."

I lean over giving her a quick kiss on the lips. With our foreheads pressed together I say, "You're mine now and I'm yours."

"I love the sound of that."

We move apart from each other, not breaking eye contact.

"Let's go to church together on Sunday." I offer. It's Wednesday night and had I not been out with her I would've gone to Bible study with Drew, Deidre and Kason. I don't get to as often as I like because some power washing jobs are done better at night when businesses are closed.

"I would like that. I attend Journey to Faith Church in Alexandria. Where do you worship?" I must have a dumbfounded look on my face because Rae says. "What? You don't like my church?"

I shake my head. "No, it's not that. I like Journey to Faith and Pastor Michael because I attend that church too."

"Really? I've been attending service there for a few years. How long have you been going?"

"My brother and his family have been attending for years and I just became a member six months ago. What service do you go to?"

"I attend the eleven o'clock service and I volunteer as an usher."

"That's why we haven't crossed paths. I attend nine o'clock." I smile thoughtfully. *God, You're showing all kinds of signs that this woman is for me.* "I can meet you for eleven am service on Sunday."

"Okay. I'm not scheduled to volunteer this week."

I reach for her hand, intertwining it with mine and placing it on the middle console. We sit quietly for a moment prolonging our time together.

Rae speaks first. "I suddenly have a taste for ice cream."

Thank God!

I pull my hand from hers to start my truck.

"Lead the way."

10

MALIK

"I love her!" Deidre whispers to me from my left.

When I told Drew and Deidre I would be attending the eleven o'clock service today instead of the nine o'clock, they became curious. I think the goofy grin I had on my face yesterday when I told them had something to do with it.

They decided to attend the eleven o'clock service too to get all up in my business. I roll with it. They might as well meet my future wife now.

Yeah, I'm claiming it.

"All this time, we have been patrons at the pharmacy and come to find out we attend the same church," Deidre says to Rae.

"You may have met her sooner if you didn't go to the drive-thru to pick up our prescriptions," Drew couldn't help throwing in.

Deidre playfully nudges him. "Don't mind my gorgeous goofball of a husband. But he's telling the truth; the drive-thru saves me time."

"No worries. That's why the drive-thru is there." Rae offers them a genuine smile before turning her eyes to me. She's standing to my right. We're all standing near one of the sanctuary doors, but not blocking the entry for others going in to find their seats. Kason had already run off with his friends to Youth Church. "Thanks for sending this guy in that day though, otherwise he and I may have never met."

I wink at her. "I have a feeling God would have made a way. If not at the pharmacy, definitely here at church." I reach over to discreetly link one of my fingers with hers.

Rae agrees. "Hmmm, you've got a point." She gives me a knowing look.

Since Wednesday when we agreed to this Christian dating thing, we've been communicating every chance we get. With my business schedule and her work schedule, this is the first we've seen each other in person since then. FaceTime has been a lifesaver. We're desperate for spending alone time together before the upcoming week keeps us busy.

"You two are so darn cute already." Deirdre grins. "Come on, let's find our seats."

We find seats on the sanctuary floor and not in the balcony. The praise and worship team lifts my spirit with their singing, then soon Pastor Michael takes the podium for his sermon.

"Everyone, please get your Bible or Bible app and go to Luke 4:17-19. I'm reading from the New International Version (NIV). Let's read." Pastor Michael looks down at the large Bible in his hand.

Rae and I both find the verse using the app on our phones. Drew and Deidre share a Bible.

"And the scroll of the prophet Isaiah was handed to Him' - *Jesus*. 'Unrolling it, He found the place where it is written:' Verse eighteen, 'The Spirit of the Lord is on me, because he has anointed me to proclaim good news to the poor. He has sent me to *proclaim freedom* for the prisoners and recovery of sight for the blind, to *set the oppressed free*.' Verse nineteen, 'to proclaim the year of the Lord's favor." Pastor Michael places his Bible on the podium.

"My topic for today is freedom! Freedom according to Jesus is: Physical, mental – emotional and spiritual. Our God, Jehovah will never put you in bondage, ever! So, He doesn't want you living a life in one. He wants you living in liberty. Unfortunately, so many Christians are not living a life of true freedom. There is something in your life that is weighting you down, keeping you in bondage. It's time you identify what that thing or things are.

"One of two things that keeps Christians in bondage is sinful habits – active or passive disobedience, conscious or not. Is there a habit in your life that you can identify that you need to repent for? In order to have full deliverance from that sin, you must ask God's forgiveness and He will *freely* give it to you. God won't make you jump through any hoops. He won't hold your sins against you. He is waiting for you to receive His deliverance from the bondage of sin.

"The second thing that keeps Christians in bondage is guilt – from past sins, past wrong doings, those coulda, shoulda, woulda's. Once you've repented for your sins, God doesn't hold it against you. In that case, you need to let it go. God is not holding you liable to it so why are you still holding on to it? Stop beating yourself up! Jesus washed your sins away with His blood. The Cross of Jesus Christ is more powerful than any sin! Your sins were nailed to the cross along with Him..."

Beside me, Rae has tears in her eyes. I reach for her hand in her lap, giving it comforting squeeze. She had revealed to me, during one of our many conversations these past few days, that she sometimes feels guilty for her miscarriages. That she may have done something wrong to cause them. And she sometimes feels guilty for getting pregnant so many times after the first miscarriage causing the loss of the babies that followed.

Of course, I told her she has no reason to feel guilty because the matter of life and death is up to God. And if she hadn't purposely done something wrong, she shouldn't hold the miscarriages against herself.

If only I can follow my own advice because I sometimes feel guilty for wasting years on Janae. An ungrateful woman. And guilty for taking too long to *fully* commit my life to Christ. Yeah, I've always been a believer – but I wasn't completely practicing my faith.

Rae looks over at me as I place her hand in my lap. I close my eyes and quietly pray. "Adonai, thank You for your love and forgiveness. Thank You for allowing Your Son Jesus to die on the Cross for our sins. Because of Him we can come to You freely. Release us of our burdens. Help us to forgive ourselves for our past mistakes as You have already forgiven us. Help us to completely accept Your love for us so we can truly see ourselves as your children. So, we can live in assurance of your grace. In Jesus name I pray..."

"Amen," Rae says along with me.

I open my eyes to find her watching me. "Thank you!" she whispers as Pastor Michael continues to preach.

From the corner of my eyes, I see Drew looking over at me holding Rae's hand with a pleased look on his face. He and Deirdre's approval of Rae further seals the deal for me. Even if it may be too soon to be thinking about forever.

11

RAE

I haven't been this nervous since I was sixteen years old and Benjamin Thompson, my secret crush, was coming over to my house for us to work on our geography project. My parents had no clue that I was in love with Benjamin – as in love as my immature self could be, when they agreed for him to come over. I obsessed over the perfect "staying at home" outfit. And making sure we had snacks and supplies for the project at our disposable. I cleaned the living room like the robot Rosie from the cartoon *The Jetsons*. I needed everything pristine.

Today I'm nervous because Malik is coming over to my condo for the first time. It's been two weeks since we've been dating and this will be his first time hanging out at my place. I went over to his apartment after church last Sunday, but just briefly for him to pick up a video game he'd purchased for his nephew to drop off on our way to brunch.

My place is never unkempt since it's only me living here. But I vacuumed and polished and scrubbed like the place was a pigsty.

Though I am nervous about being alone with Malik where there's a bed nearby, I also have peace with him being in my space.

He calms me.

Greg was my category five hurricane; Malik is my peace after the storm.

The sound of the doorbell brings me out of my head. I look over the dishes on the kitchen counter. I prepared homemade Chipotle. Brown rice, since it's mine and Malik's favorite, grilled chicken and steak tips, salsa and guacamole that I bought fresh from the grocery store, sour cream and cheese. We both know beans aren't our best friends so it's off the menu.

Pleased that everything is in its place, I head towards the front door.

I look down at my black yoga pants and yellow shirt, ensuring no stains before I unlock the door.

"Hey," I greet Malik with a wide smile. I give my eyes the pleasure of sweeping over him dressed in grey joggers and a white t-shirt.

Gawd! How am I supposed to keep my hands to myself with him looking good enough to eat? *Help your daughter, Lord.*

"Hey baby, I brought wine." He presents the bottle of red wine from behind his back.

I open the door wider, welcoming him inside. After shutting and locking the door, Malik tilts my chin up with his fingers then presses his lips sensually against my mine. I moan despite the warning bells in my head already letting me know we need to cool it.

Malik breaks the kiss first. He looks at me with fire of desire in his eyes. "Let's eat what you prepared before I have *you* for dinner instead," he unabashedly lets me know.

For a moment, I forget why we can't just rip each other's clothes off.

"Keep looking at me like that and we'll both be repenting in the morning."

I bite down on my lip.

Malik groans then takes my hand, heading towards the kitchen which is easy to find in the open floor plan of my condo.

With our bowls heaped high with food, we eat sitting across from each other at the kitchen island. We chat about how our days went then move on to other topics.

"Drew and Deidre are a cute couple. It's good to see a married couple still in like and in love with each other after fifteen years of marriage. Them running their accounting business together must be part of the secret."

"Yeah. They got married young. I remember my mom being upset with Drew because he wanted to get married while he was in college. She wanted him to focus on his education first. Dad was cool with it, but he did try to talk Drew into at least waiting until after he got his college degree. And I honestly thought he was stupid for wanting to tie himself down to one woman so soon. He told me he found a good woman and he refused to let her go...that's what I feel when I'm with you." Malik looks at me from across the island with a determined look on his face.

Goosebumps pop up along my arms. "You already see yourself marrying me?" I pick up my glass of wine to take a sip, trying to hide the way his words affect me.

"I wouldn't waste your time or mine if I wasn't sure before I asked to date you. I was engaged to Janae but...with you, I confidently see forever."

"I have been married before and divorced partly because I can't have children. Are you sure you can accept the fact that I won't be able to give you kids? That's something you may regret or resent me for. We're only two weeks into this, so it won't be hard to end it now…" I swallow the lump in my throat.

"It won't be easy for me to walk away from you. And I know it won't be easy for you either. I'm falling in love with you Rae, and ain't nothing you can do to stop it."

Air pushes from my lungs that I didn't realize I was holding. "I'm falling in love with you too and it's too darn soon." I giggle to hide my nervousness.

Malik chuckles, reaching across the kitchen island for my hand, linking our fingers together. "You're stuck with me, babe."

"In that case, we need to come up with a plan to deal with sexual temptation until you make an honest woman out of me one day."

"What sexual temptation?" Malik teases with laughter in his eyes.

"Boy, you know exactly what I'm talking about. We're both grown and experienced with sex. And this is the first for both of us abstaining. How can I keep myself from *sitting* on your lap?"

The laughter in his eyes turns to desire. He closes them briefly to regain himself. Looking back at me he says, "We'll make a deal to pray out loud when the temptation gets too strong."

"What if my prayer is – *yes, God!*?" I'm partially joking.

Malik groans. "Rae..." The plea in his voice has me ready to pray out loud – now. Witnessing his restraint is sexy in and of itself. "We both have to try to be strong. But if one of us is weak, the other has to be stronger."

I willingly relent. "Okay."

"Now that we have established ground rules, I better help you with these dishes then leave." Malik pushes away from the counter and stands, picking up his dish then mine.

As much as I would like for him to stay longer – it's probably best he leaves. I don't think there's enough prayers I can say out loud to save me tonight. And like the Good Book says – practice self-control.

12

RAE

I can't help the smile on my face as I count pills into the dispenser. Next to my workstation at the pharmacy is a boutique of yellow roses that was delivered a few hours ago.

Malik.

This man is my weakness. I had absolutely no intentions of getting into another relationship after my divorce months ago. It's hard not to believe in love…happily ever after…again when it comes to Malik.

He makes it seem so easy to go all in. Risk it all. To be vulnerable.

I'm still cautious though, because Greg appeared to be the perfect man for me until he wasn't. He became the absolute worst. My enemy.

Now here is Malik – sending me flowers because today is the anniversary of my last miscarriage. Zariah's third heavenly birthday. Greg never remembered any or gave any indication that he did. Quite frankly, I mourned in silence to avoid dealing with him.

"Hmmm, I want whatever Malik has been putting on you 'cause you've been smiling like a Cheshire cat all morning." Yasmine breaks my concentration.

"He's not putting anything on me. He's a thoughtful, God fearing, hardworking, respectable man that I like a *lot*."

"Yeah and he's fine too! You two have been dating for a month. No way y'all haven't been down and dirty yet."

Thankfully there are no customers waiting to fill or pickup prescriptions. Which technically is the only time we freely talk like this.

"Not that it's any of your business – but we're abstaining."

Yasmine doesn't have a quick response which makes me look up to see a blank expression on her face. "Like abstaining for the three-month rule or...until marriage?"

"Marriage." My focus goes back to filling a prescription and inputting the data.

"Really? I don't know if I can abstain from sex, not when I know how good it is...well how good it can be with the right partner. You sure Malik isn't gay?"

I guess that's a valid question. Unfortunately, in today's time a man willingly abstaining from sex would be considered suspect. A definite abnormality. Either he's on the downlow, had a sex change or his pipes don't work.

Malik is heterosexual, born a male, and I've seen the pipes through his pants – they work. Well!

"He's straight!" I keep the facts to myself. "Honestly, I'm praying to God I can hold out. I've never *purposely* abstained from sex. Before I was married, I went months without sex because I wasn't in a relationship. It's different now that I'm dating Malik and telling myself no. It helps that we're both in agreement of honoring our faith."

I can't help but recall the Scripture Psalms 16:32. *"Better a patient person than a warrior, one with self-control than one who takes a city."* We can wait.

"That's noble and all – but when I get that urge, I need to handle it. ASAP. Find me a one-night stand if I must to deal with that situation."

Being the unofficial big sister, I reply, "I get your point, just be safe. There are way too many STDs, unwanted pregnancies and baby daddy – baby mama drama going on. People having children with people they shouldn't have even had sex with."

It's crazy the amount of prescriptions we fill for STDs. The epidemic should be enough to scare people into practicing celibacy, apart from it being Biblical. It's almost comical that people like me and Malik that are abstaining are sometimes seen as weird, when those casually having sex are exposing themselves to too many diseases and unnecessary drama.

"I am...but now that I think about it, I do need to take the morning-after pill." Yasmine whispers the last part.

My fingers stop moving across the computer keyboard. "Yasmine," I chastise in a whisper. "If you're practicing safe sex, why do you need the pill?"

Her eyes shift away from me. "The condom broke and I missed my appointment for my birth control shot."

The sound of a car horn at the drive-thru window stops my reply to Yasmine. I turn around to smile at the elderly, Hispanic woman.

From behind me Yasmine says, "Take care of that. I'm taking a fifteen-minute break to handle *that* situation."

I pray Yasmine doesn't get herself caught up in a situation she will regret.

Fifteen minutes later, Yasmine is back from her break. She walks up to the table where she was data checking and bagging prescriptions earlier. I had finished assisting the woman at the window. Two other customers came to the counter to drop off prescriptions while she was gone.

"I'm sorry, Rae. I hope I didn't offend you taking the emergency contraceptive."

I had finally come around to telling Yasmine about my miscarriages. "I'm not offended. Just don't put yourself in that position again because you had casual sex. A few minutes of physical gratification with the wrong person can carry a lifelong problem if you're not careful."

Yasmine nods thoughtfully. "You're right about that. I don't even know dude's last name that I hooked up with last night. And no matter how good he was, I don't want a baby by him."

A white man approaches the pharmacy counter, stopping our conversation. Yasmine turns her attention to him, greeting him professionally.

My cellphone vibrates in my lab coat pocket indicating a text notification. I pull it out and cringe, seeing who the text is from. I can't wait to delete Greg's number from my phone after we close on the sale of the house, which will be later today. He finally agreed with me on accepting an offer closest to the sale price.

Mistake: Make sure you are on time for the closing.

I roll my eyes reading his message. At the last second, before returning phone to my coat pocket, I send a response instead of ignoring him like I usually do.

Rae: Of course. I'll finally be done with you.

I smile. I'm probably poking the bear, but today marks the beginning of getting Greg completely out of my life. I can't be happier. We won't have to communicate ever again.

Mistake: Having an incomplete woman like you as my wife wasn't fun either.

I shake my head. If his only insult to me is my lack of birthing children, I'll let him have that jab.

Mistake: Good luck finding a man that wants a bitter, broken woman like you.

Rae: See you at 3:30 □

Malik will be picking me up at 3:00pm to take me to the realtor's office for 3:30pm. This morning, he met me at the car dealership where I left my car to get the tires rotated and oil changed.

I can't wait to see my man. A good man. Greg needs to see that I can do phenomenal without him.

13

MALIK

I love experiencing the change of seasons – specifically autumn. Here in the Washington DC metro area, during this time of year, the leaves on trees change colors from green to red, yellow, brown, eventually falling in heaps on the ground.

October is one of the most profitable times of year for Precise Cuts Landscaping, apart from spring and summer months. Most people hate raking, bagging and hauling leaves off their property. Honestly – I don't enjoy it either as the one hired to do the tasks. The money, however? I enjoy it much! Which is why Saint is helping me complete my landscaping jobs today. I have two and half more hours of work before I need to pick up Rae from work to take her to her appointment.

"A'ight Malik, so check this. Marley wants me to drop the other women on my roster before she agrees to me taking her out on a fourth date. She's saying the first three dates were a test run to see if we have chemistry and connected on an intellectual level. But now that her feelings are getting heavily involved, she doesn't want to compete with anyone else." He looks over at me with a perplexed look on his face while pushing some of the leaves we gathered into a recycling bag. We're in DC at Judea's sister Jada's Bed and Breakfast.

Saint has attended a few Wednesday night Bible studies with me, but has yet to attend a Sunday service because he's either hung over from partying the night before or he has a warm body in bed next to him. On one occasion at Bible study, he made true to his word of hooking up with a "Christian chick" – Marley.

I stop picking up a handful of leaves to address him. "The fact that you took Marley on one date, let alone three, potentially four, speaks volume. You're really into her. Three months and she's turned you out and she didn't have to give up the booty to do so." As long as I've known Saint, I can't recall him willingly taking a girl out on a date.

Saint tries to deny it. "Man, I'm not sweating no woman." He bends to continue picking up the raked leaves in his gloved hands and shoves them into the bag.

"Saint, we boys, right?" I don't wait for him to agree. "Don't try play me. You're into her. The dates and the fact you haven't dropped her since she asked you to axe the other women you're messing with tells me everything I need to know."

"Okay, yeah I'm really feeling her. But I've never been with just one woman – exclusively. I get she's a Christian and all. But didn't Jacob and them in the Bible have more than one woman?"

"They did, but that was in the Old Testament, before Jesus. Before the New Covenant. I doubt Marley is going to fall for your beliefs of having multiple women. And you've got to respect her standards. If she was seeing multiple dudes, how would you feel?"

Saint's jaw clenches. I knew I would strike a nerve. Any man that's one hundred percent interested in a woman does not want her even looking at another man, let alone entertaining one.

"I would crack their skulls," he says matter of factly. "Damn! This must be how you feel about Rae." He shakes his head. "Oh my God! Please tell me Marley will not withhold the pussy until marriage. Three months of dating has been torture enough. Imma end up wifing her before the year's out." He looks stressed.

I laugh. Hard. *Welcome to the club brother. But it will be worth it.* I don't say it out loud. I know he's going to need time to mentally process the new feelings he's feeling for Marley.

After getting my business done for the day, I arrive at the pharmacy to pick up Rae fifteen minutes before she's scheduled to clock out. I use the time sitting in my truck to check business emails. Later this evening, I must create and email a few invoices. I smile thoughtfully as I read an email message for a business review, I received on one of the few small business job leads websites I use.

★★★★★**Malik Day, owner of Precise Cuts Landscaping, was a joy to work with. He is very professional. He promptly emailed me a quote for power washing my home and creating a new flowerbed. He delivered as promised in a timely manner. My house is so clean it looks brand new and I absolutely adore my new** flowerbed. I have told all my new neighbors about his services. I'm sure they will be calling him soon. I will definitely be using Mr. Day's services again.

I'm so engrossed in reading and responding to emails that I didn't notice Rae walking out of the pharmacy. I look over to the driver's side window where she's standing, knocking on the window to get my attention. A broad smile breaks out on my face. That happens often when I'm near her. I unlock the door for her to climb in.

"Sorry about that, babe," I hold up my cellphone. "I was responding to emails." I lean over to give her a kiss after she's in the seat.

Rae strokes the hair on my jaw. I love it when she does that. "It's okay. Thank you for picking me up." She smiles against my lips. "I missed you."

I press my lips against hers one more time before saying, "I missed you too."

We pull apart and I start the truck.

"Tonight, after you take me to pick up my car. I'm going to the store to buy groceries to cook you dinner."

Dang, I'm feeling like I just won the lotto. My girl can throw down in the kitchen. Her home cooking is always a treat. "I need to be your chauffeur more often if this is the reward."

"You being *you* is the reason." I feel her reaching for my hand on the center console. I briefly take my eyes off the road to watch her clasps her fingers with mine. I can feel the vein on her wrist and it's pulsing fast. "Malik, I love you."

My head jerks back towards her while my foot slams on the brakes. On the highway.

"Malik!" Rae shrieks.

My eyes lift to look in the rearview mirror. A car is speeding towards us on the two-lane highway.

Taking my foot off the brakes I quickly merge to the left shoulder, then place the truck in park.

I unbuckle Rae's seatbelt then gently tug her over to me. It's easy for her to climb over the console in her black slacks and cheetah print flats. I push the middle console up to give her more room to straddle me. Not caring that we're parked on the side of the road at 3pm in the afternoon, I cup Rae's face before deeply kissing her lips. I make love to her mouth the way I desperately want to her body.

"I love you, Rae." I kiss her cheeks, her chin, her neck. "I love you."

"You don't think it's too soon?" She's concerned for no reason.

I shake my head. "There's no timeframe for when a person falls in love. For some people it takes weeks, months or years. All I care about is that you love me." She nods.

I caress her neck. "And I love you. My love for you grows stronger every day. Best believe I'm gone love you like you've never been loved before."

"Please and thank you!" Rae strokes my beard.

"I got you." I peck her lips with mine. "We better leave before PG county police pulls up with you over here trying to take advantage of me."

We both laugh as she moves off my lap and back into her seat.

I park in front of the building of the title company for Rae's 3:30 appointment. I get out of the truck first to open the door for her. The door to the entrance of the building opens and a goofy looking, light-skinned dude in a suit steps out.

"Who the hell are you?" This clown asks me. Rae doesn't have to say anything for me to know this is her ex – Greg.

"Her man that treats her better than you ever did! Need to know anything else?" *Like how my fist feels against your jaw?*

Greg flexes like he's about to do something. Christian or not, I will body him on the spot. I'm itching to knock him out for what he's put Rae through.

I feel Rae's hand on my arm. My fist relaxes because of the contact. I shoot missiles at Greg with my eyes before turning to look at the woman who has captured my heart.

"Babe, I'll meet you here when I'm done. Closing shouldn't take long." This is the first time Rae has called me by a pet name and I'm not sure if it's just for show or if she means it. I like it either way.

I lift her chin to kiss her on the lips. "Okay, I'll be waiting. Let me know if he says or does anything out of pocket."

Old dude is still standing there watching. It must be killing him to see Rae move on. Good for me he didn't realize he had a good woman. I'm the man of Rae's life now.

I swat Rae on the butt as she steps away. She giggles looking over her shoulder at me, blowing me a kiss. Greg finally gets the hint, walking back inside the office building. I stay away from touching Rae inappropriately – it's part of our boundaries to maintain our celibacy – but I needs Greg to know she's *mine*.

I get back in my truck to wait for Rae. *God, you sent her to me, now help me to be all the man she needs, 'cause I already know she's all the woman for me.*

I hope I don't have to remind Greg that I'm her man.

14

MALIK

Eight months later, me and Rae's love is still going strong. Tonight, we're going out to dinner with Drew and Deidre. Saint is joining us as well with one of the three women in his life.

Rae is breathtaking in her red, tight fitting knee high dress and nude heels. It looks like she straightened her soft coarse hair for the night which has my fingers twitching to run through her strands. My baby is forty years old and killing the body goals and fashion game. I had to pray out loud when she opened the door when I came to pick her up. I was ready to throw her over my shoulder and march to her bedroom. Only by the grace of God, we've made it through nine months of dating without succumbing to our flesh. Being a part of the singles' ministry at church has been helpful.

We ride in Rae's car for the night instead of my pickup truck with my work materials in it. I pull up to the front of the swanky restaurant in DC to valet park.

"Did I tell you how handsome you look tonight?" Rae asks once I take her hand to enter the restaurant.

In celebration of the one hundred and twenty thousand a year government contract I landed for landscaping several Maryland government agencies, I rented a designer suit for the occasion. And damn, ya boy looks good. At least according to Rae, because she's said so several times since I picked her up.

"I think you may have mentioned it." I wink at her.

"Father, when I am weak, You are strong!" Rae prays, causing me to chuckle.

"The man of the hour," Drew stands when Rae and I approach the table. Deidre stands too, along with Saint and his girl, Tashina, I believe this one's name is. I can't keep track of them like he does. Everyone is dressed to the nines tonight.

"Thank you!" I let them all know after they congratulate me.

Minutes later, we're enjoying appetizers and our drinks. Drew said he's picking up the tab in my honor for which I'm thankful. Business is doing well but I still don't want to spend frivolously. In order to fulfill the government contract, I hired two lawn care companies as sub-contractors. I still will make a good profit from the deal, and it frees me up to fulfill my other business obligations.

"Why do you keep checking your phone?" Saint's date, whose name is actually Trina not Tashina, snaps loudly at him, distracting me from my conversation.

Sitting to my left, Saint gives Trina a look that mothers give their children when they say or do something out of line. "I'm not your man, therefore you have no right to question me," he evenly replies to her.

Trina fixes her mouth to say something back but decides against it, clamming her mouth shut. I can't really feel bad for her because she knew the deal in regards to hooking up with him from the beginning and decided to go along with it.

"I'll be right back," I tell Rae who's sitting to my right. She, Deidre, Drew and I were discussing the sad state of R&B music today. Rae nods, going back into the conversation.

I turn to Saint, "Bruh, let me talk to you for a minute."

When Saint and I near the bar area where there aren't many people around, I ask, "What's going on with you? You've been staring at your phone like your life is on the line."

He looks down at said cellphone in his hand. "It's Marley's birthday today, man. I left her a voice message and sent her a birthday text this morning and she hasn't replied yet."

I must not be hearing him right. "Wait, Marley from church? Marley who volunteers on the usher board with Rae? The same Marley you dropped eight months ago because she wanted you to give her the respect of being the only woman in your life?"

He huffs a breath. "Yeah, that Marley."

"Why are you sweating whether she contacts you back or not? You chose Trina and them over her."

"Cause out of all the women I've been with, she's the only one that...that I really care about."

"Then why are you here with Trina?"

"Because Trina gives up the goods when and where I need it without me putting a ring on her finger and committing myself to life."

"And how is that working out for you? You act like you don't even want to sit near Trina, much less have sex with her later."

"Oh, I'm hitting it later, trust! But that's all I need Trina for. Marley's the whole package though. I enjoyed hanging out with her, talking about nothing and everything and to be honest, I think if and when I ever do have sex with her, I wouldn't want no one else."

"Yet when she asked you for commitment, you let her go. And she already told you nothing is going on below the belt until she's a married woman."

Saint huffs, running his hand over his freshly twisted dreads. "And that's why I dropped her. Can you honestly see me committing to one woman?" He looks horrified.

"Yeah, I can. It may be hard at first for you, but committing yourself to one woman is not a death sentence – especially if it's the right woman. The one God has for you. You'll still find other women attractive, but you can commit in your heart to only respond to one. And from what I see, you got a beautiful woman at the table waiting for you, but your heart is with the one who hasn't responded to your text. You're scared bro, but imagine how heartbroken you'll be if you let the perfect woman for you get away because you're afraid of manning up. You're almost forty. How much longer you want to play the field? 'Cause at this point – you're not winning." I pat him on the shoulder.

"Man Malik, I'm not like you and Drew. I see you devoted to one woman and I'm not gonna lie – I want that too. But I've been juggling multiple women for years..." He shakes his head. "This is who I am."

"Nah, that's the lie the enemy wants you to believe. Now is not the time or place for me to break it all down for you, but as a believer in Christ, you become a new man. Born again. And I guarantee you are a man that can love and be faithful to one woman and she will be in return to you. I'll talk to you more about it later, aight?"

Saint nods.

"Let's get back to the table."

Dinner is served and the conversation about the state of R&B music continues.

"Who do you think is a better singer – Tyrese or Jamie Foxx?" Deidre asks Trina and Rae.

Rae speaks first, "Jamie."

Trina replies, "Tyrese."

"Man, both of them dudes can't sing!" Saint claims before putting a fork full of prime rib into his mouth.

"Oh, be quiet, Saint. You're just hating 'cause you sound like Shabaka from Star Wars when you try to sing a note. Anyway..." Deidre turns her attention back to the ladies. "Jamie Foxx is hands down the better singer..."

I tune out of their conversation, enjoying my prime rib, rice and mixed vegetables. Across the table, Drew gives me a knowing look before shifting his eyes to Rae sitting beside me. When Drew looks back at me, I nod. My heart starts beating fast like a drum during Junkanoo parade in The Bahamas. My nerves had been settled most of the night, but with just his small gesture, Drew has me nervous.

"Hey, Marley!" Rae exclaims, pushing her chair back to stand.

I hear the loud sound of metal hitting a porcelain plate. I look over at Saint who dropped the fork from his hand. He's looking over my shoulder with love in his eyes. Aww man, my boy has got it bad. I can relate.

"Happy birthday girl!" Rae and Marley hug each other. After the exchange, Rae turns to our table. "Everyone, you know Marley from church. Trina, Marley attends the same church as us. Saint…" Rae voice trails off. I turn my neck to see Saint staring at Marley with so much admiration.

Everyone, except perhaps Trina, knows that Marley and Saint went on a few dates months ago.

Marley waves. "Hi everyone."

After we greet her, there's an awkward silence. Our eyes are ping-ponging between Saint and Marley. The chemistry between them is insane. Even Trina must suspect something.

"Hey Marley, are you ready?" a tall, basketball type looking dude walks up behind Marley.

"Yes." Marley says to dude. Then to us, "You all enjoy the rest of your night. Bye."

Dude places his hand on the small of Marley's back to guide her towards the area the hostess is taking them to be seated.

Saint abruptly pushes back from the table. "She's on a date? And with that goofy looking dude?" Now that the love haze Marley had him under is broken, he's piping mad.

I grip Saint by his wrist before he can stand and raise hell in here tonight. Because I already see the storm in his eyes. I lean close so only he can hear. "Bro, I promise you, if you mess this night up for me, I'm telling all your chicks you have herpes. Then I will personally crack your skull!" I grit through my teeth.

This night is too important to me for Saint to ruin because he was too scared to give up the frivolous women in his life for a dime-piece.

Saint settles back into his seat while closing his eyes. I guess he's getting his mind right – and he better be.

"Is he going to be okay?" Rae whispers in my ear.

I nod. "He'll get over it, for now. I'm going to talk some sense into him tomorrow."

Rae nods then turns sympathetic eyes over to Trina. Trina is visibly shaking with what I presume is anger because the temperature in the restaurant isn't frigid.

"It was nice meeting you all, but I have to leave." Trina snatches her tiny clutch off the table, stands and storms off.

Saint opens his eyes, but doesn't immediately move to go after her. Deidre and Rae try to decide which one of them or both should go see after Trina.

"I'll check on Trina. It's not fair to her that I have interest in another woman when she's my guest for tonight." Saint leaves the table.

I send up silent prayers – one particularly for the fact that it seems Saint is manning up and taking responsibility for the poor way he's been treating Trina – tonight and otherwise.

"Here's a toast to my hardworking man! I love you babe and I know God is going to continue to bless your business. Congratulations on this new deal and here's to many more to come. Cheers!" Rae raises her glass filled with champagne and we all, less Trina, follow suit, clinking our glasses together.

"Thank you, baby." I place my drink down on the table and shift in my seat to fully face Rae. "This success wouldn't be as special without you in my life. Thank you for encouraging me and being my unofficial secretary – helping me fill out government forms, sending out invoices and ordering supplies. In nine months, my life has been better with you in it…"

I shove my hand in my pants pocket to pull out the velvet box. Rae gasps when she sees it, but even more so when I push back my chair and get on my knee. "Rae Evangeline Cooper, will you do me the honor of being my wife?"

"Oh my God! Yes!" Rae cups my bearded cheeks before placing kisses all over my face which causes me to chuckle. "I would love to be your wife."

Deidre, Drew and Saint cheer, along with a few spectators near our table in the restaurant.

I pull back from Rae's embrace to open the ring box revealing the perfect size diamond for her delicate finger.

Rae's eyes widen in shock and joy. "Malik…the ring is beautiful. Perfect."

I take her hand and slip the ring on her finger. "Thank you for agreeing to be my wife. I love you."

"Of course. I would be a fool to say no. I love you."

I kiss Rae as decently as I can in public.

"Congratulations!!!" Deidre gets out of her seat to hug Rae then me. "Malik you did good with the ring."

"Congratulations! Rae, thank you for putting Malik out of his misery. He's had that ring for weeks and has been freaking out on whether or not you would accept his proposal."

Drew was with me when I purchased the three-carat, white gold ring. I spent a whole lot of more G's and put more thought into this ring than I did the one I purchased Janae. Which further confirmed how much in love I am with Rae.

Saint decides to throw in his two cents. "Yes, thank God! Malik has been acting like you would say no and have him crying like a baby." He laughs and we all follow suit.

"Man, y'all shut up!" I playfully snap on them.

Rae gently tugs on my beard. "You had nothing to be worried about. I know in my heart that you are the one for me. I have never felt the type of love we share before. You treat me with respect, admiration and love. I'm so happy when I'm with you."

"I can't wait for you to be my wife." I hug her against my side.

"Me too."

15

RAE

"It's been months since I've been able to see my feet over this belly. But this cushioned stool is a godsend. I wouldn't have been able to work seven months pregnant without it." Yasmine eases her pregnant body on the cushioned stool at the pharmacy counter.

The emergency contraceptive Yasmine took eight months ago worked – but a month later she had another one-night stand which resulted in her getting pregnant.

I fight the emotion of envy. Envy of the fact that she's able to carry her unborn child much further along than I was able to for all my babies.

"The Lord will work out his plans for my life— for your faithful love, O Lord, endures forever. Don't

abandon me, for you made me." Psalms 138:8 reminds me that despite my not being able to have children, the Lord's plans for my life will still be manifested. I will not envy another person's life. What God has for me is what is best for my life.

Busy counting pills, I lift my head briefly to look over at Yasmine. "You are carrying Yasir well." I admire her pregnant body. All her baby weight is in her belly. With her being in her late twenties, I have no doubt she'll bounce back to her pre-pregnancy weight in no time after she gives birth to her son. "And you haven't had any pregnancy related problems. That's a blessing."

Yasmine rubs her swollen midsection. "Yeah. No pregnancy issues other than baby daddy mess." She shakes her head in disgust. "Ayaan still hasn't told his folks that he's having a son. He's afraid of what they will think of him getting a half-black woman he'd only met three hours before pregnant. And he's still insisting that he wants a DNA test to prove Yasir is his. Oh, and he hates the name Yasir – but that's his problem because that's the name going on the birth certificate."

Yasmine's baby father is Indian. Apparently, Ayaan's family is strict on not dating outside of their race. Add the fact that Ayaan is having an illegitimate child – equals he's got himself in a tough predicament.

Yasmine too. She's having a child with a man she barely knows, from a different culture and religious practices. Yasmine has Christian beliefs – a total opposite of Ayaan's Hindu beliefs.

I honestly don't know what to tell her. I pray God's will be done regarding the situation. Yasir is a blessing from the Lord, despite the circumstances.

"Don't allow it to stress you out. You have my godson in there. I don't want him to develop any complications because you're stressed," I sincerely respond. I can't wait to spoil him rotten. Yasmine and I have gotten really close as friends. I consider her a sister I always wanted.

"I refuse to let Ayaan stress me out. I would hate to raise Yasir by myself because he will need his father too, but I will if Ayaan leaves me no other choice."

I've been thinking about Yasmine's predicament all day. Which makes it no surprise that when Malik and I sit before our pre-marriage counselor, Dr. Danesha Culmer, the topic of children is brought up.

I twist my engagement ring around on my finger – a habit I have when I'm uncomfortable. This is me and Malik's fourth session with Dr. Culmer where we have easily discussed numerous topics regarding marriage and relationship. Today's topic, however, makes me nervous for numerous reasons.

"I can't have children," I swallow the pain the four words evoke inside of me. Greg's hurtful remarks regarding my lack of childbearing bombard my mind no matter how much I try to bury them for good.

One of the most important things a woman is supposed to be good at and you can't even carry a baby past three months. Worthless!

Would Malik grow to feel the same way about me soon?

I feel Malik reach for my left hand, rubbing his thumb in circles in the palm of my hand. He had picked up on my nervous habit some time ago.

"You can have children," Malik says affirmatively. I start to pull my hand away from his grasp, but he holds my hand still in my lap. "I believe in my heart that she can give birth to our babies." He tells Dr. Culmer.

Malik called me one morning weeks ago about a dream he had of me carrying our baby to full term and giving birth to a healthy baby boy. He was so excited and said he believes it was a sign from God.

After the phone call, I cried. Cried until my eyes were red and puffy. Cried because despite my faith, I cannot believe in the possibility of me having children of my own. I cried because no matter how much I love Malik and want to be his wife – I think I must let him go.

It will destroy me if he later resents me like Greg did.

Dr. Culmer's face and tone remains neutral as she speaks. "I admire your faith in Rae being able to give birth to your future children. However, you are aware of her history with pregnancy."

Dr. Culmer turns her eyes on me. "What do you think about this, Rae?"

Like a movie preview reel, all my miscarriage experiences play in the forefront of my mind. I squeeze my eyes shut to block the pain.

"No! I...I can't." I exclaim loudly for both the bad memories and not wanting to put my body through that strain ever again. I don't want to mourn losing another child – ever.

I feel Malik's body tense beside me on the couch. "You don't want to have my children...our children?"

This is the first time we're *really* talking about this.

"I can't put my body through that again. And I don't know if I will survive losing another baby." I turn my head to look at my fiancé. "I would give anything to have your baby...our baby, but my body won't."

"But my dream. And our faith in God, trusting and believing that He can work a miracle in our lives." He looks so hopeful.

"Malik," I groan. "I have faith in God too, but I've had five miscarriages. You have no idea how difficult that is mentally, physically and emotionally. I won't put myself through that again, not even for you."

And just like that, I kill the hope in his dark brown eyes. When I pull my hand out of his grasp, he does not stop me.

"Would you two consider other options for having children, like a surrogate or adoption?" Dr. Culmer asks, cutting through the sudden tension in the room.

Malik answers first. "I'm okay with a surrogate as a second option."

"I would need more time to think about surrogacy. I'm not sure how I would handle watching another woman carry and give birth to my child." I reply.

"Does that mean adoption would be your first choice?" Dr. Culmer asks me.

I shake my head. "I don't know."

"Do you want to have children? You haven't said otherwise before, but now..." I can hear the doubt in Malik's voice...about us having kids...about us.

I know he is hurt, but I can't handle this right now. It's all too real. Too painful.

"All I know is, I can't physically give birth to a child and I don't want to try again to experience the pain and loss for the eleventh time. Obviously, I'm not completely healed from my experiences because the thought of watching another woman nurture my baby in her womb and give birth to my child and share such a remarkable experience every mother should have with their baby is too much for me to handle right now. And adoption is a lot more complicated and can come with a whole lot of heartbreak that my heart is not set up to handle anymore."

"Which means you don't want us to try to have children? I understand the pain you've experienced, and I wish I could take it all away. I went into this relationship knowing your past, but I thought we both were willing to explore other options for having children."

I shift on the couch to turn my body towards Malik. "All I'm saying is that I need time to fully process our options for children. Okay?"

Malik searches my face before replying, "Okay."

This is our first pre-marital counselling session where I left the meeting unsure about everything.

I don't ever want to hate Malik like I do Greg…becoming his wife may allow that to happen.

16

MALIK

"You look like hell. Sit. Let me at least get your hair looking tight." Saint pats his barber chair, indicating for me to sit down. I have an appointment same day and time every three weeks, so he's been expecting me.

I'm glad these appointments are at eight in the morning when the shop is usually quiet. I'm not in the mood for chopping it up with a bunch of men and a few women that frequent the barber shop. My mind has been heavy for two days since me and Rae's pre-martial therapy session. Things are feeling off between us. Rae hasn't called me, and I haven't called her. We have only communicated via text messaging. It's the basic, *good morning, how are you, good night. I love you.*

In all the time we've been dating and engaged, I have not once felt doubt about us like I do now.

Can I marry a woman who doesn't want children? Because that's basically what I got from our therapy session. I love Rae more than I have loved any woman. Honestly – I think she's the only woman I have ever loved romantically. The feelings I had for Janae are nothing compared to the feelings I have for Rae.

But can I marry her knowing she doesn't want children? She's forty, I'm thirty-seven – kids are still a good possibility for us at our ages. It's July and we have a destination wedding date set for November, right before the Thanksgiving holiday, on the beach in Florida. Then plans to fly out to The Turks and Caicos for our honeymoon the next day.

I have literally been counting down the days to Rae becoming my wife – my good thing.

Now?

I don't know.

"What's up with you, man?" Saint drapes the cape around me before snapping it in place around my neck.

I scratch my scruffy beard contemplating. "Rae doesn't want to have children...or at least try to." I knew about her struggles when we started dating and accepted them – but that dream I had about her having our baby felt so real. Like it was a message from God.

"Damn, bro. I know you always wanted a lil' dude or shortie that looks like you." Saint preps my hair for the cut. "Even I'm ready for a seed. Marley got my nose so wide open, I'm ready to have a lil' football team if she willing to carry them all nine months at a time. And at this rate, the second I make her my wife and we consummate I may mess around and get her pregnant with quadruplets." He chuckles.

Saint made the right decision to let go of the three women he was juggling to date Marley exclusively. Seeing her out with another man made things perfectly clear for him.

"Yeah, I've wanted at least one kid. But now that may never happen."

"Is it because of her age? She's forty, but that isn't too old to have children."

"No...she's..." I stress over telling him her business, but I do want to hear his advice. "She's had a few miscarriages in the past and doesn't want to chance putting her body through that anymore."

"I can understand that..."

I do too. And I also have hope for God's miracle.

"...I mean...look. Y'all aren't married yet. Why don't you just get another chick pregnant. Simple. That way you can have your kid and Rae without walking around here looking a science experiment."

"Man, that's got to be the dumbest advice you could give. How would getting another chick pregnant solve my problem?"

"Rae doesn't want to have children because she's afraid of having another miscarriage. So have a baby with someone else. You and Rae get married and you co-parent with baby moms."

I actually consider it for 3.5 seconds. I shake my head. "No. I love Rae. I wouldn't do that to her."

"What are you going to do about not having a kid? Can you marry Rae knowing she doesn't want to have children?"

And we're back to square one.

Saint picks up his clippers. "I know you got a lot on your mind, so tonight we're going out to shoot the breeze." He doesn't wait for my response before turning on the clippers to get my fade and beard shaped to perfection.

I take Saint up on his offer to meet him at The Spot at 7pm. The situation with me and Rae is starting to stress me out, especially since I finally called Rae twenty minutes ago and she acted like she didn't want to be bothered by me.

"Malik." Rae's tone was dry, unlike the pleasant voice I was usually greeted with when we spoke.

"Hey, how was your day?"

"Okay."

"Are you home?"

"Yeah."

"Can I come over? You want me to bring dinner?"

"No."

Rae's short answers and unpleasant tone were beginning to piss me off.

"Does your attitude have anything to do with our therapy session?"

"No."

"Then what's up?"

"Nothing!"

Lord give me strength! *"Rae. I'm trying hard to understand what's going on because you and I both know this attitude you have isn't your usual self. And if it's about us having children then let's talk, but please stop with the passive aggressive, one-word answer, nonsense."*

"I'm busy, Malik. Okay."

"Busy doing what?"

"Busy taking time for myself. Can we talk another time?"

I sigh deeply. "Are you upset because I'm just calling after two days?" You haven't bothered to call me either.

"No."

"Okay, bye! Have all the me time you need." I hung up but regretted it immediately. My pride stopped me from calling her back.

"Here, a cold one on me." Saint places a cold, bottled beer in front of me on the table. We're in the game area in The Spot watching a few people play pool before we take our turn at the pool table.

"Thanks," I offer before taking a swig.

"I take it you're still trying to figure out your dilemma?" Saint eases into the seat next to me.

"I'm more confused than ever. But I'm not here to talk about my problems." I need tonight to be a distraction from my uncertain love life and pending marriage.

"I hear ya. Which means I won't take pity on you on the pool table."

I shake my head and smile. This dude thinks he's a better pool player than me. "Saint, you have never beat me at pool. What makes you think tonight is any different?"

"Negro, please! I know you got some personal problems right now that may be clogging your memory, but I've whooped your ass a few times."

He may be right. I chuckle. "Man, whatever!"

Minutes later, Saint is indeed whooping my behind at the pool table. I blame it on my clouded mind and uncertainty about my relationship with Rae. Also, the ladies watching us play pool have me slightly distracted – the few beers I've drunk play a role too. I'm not drunk though. Just mellow.

I call it quits around nine.

"Want some company tonight?" A dark-skinned beauty asks as I'm making my way towards the exit. When I turn to look at her, I see Saint over her shoulder giving me the thumbs up. I wonder if he encouraged her to follow me. He can't be serious about me sleeping with a complete stranger, getting her pregnant, to solve my baby dilemma. The irony is, Saint is on his way to meet up with his now one and only, Marley – who he's practicing celibacy with. How is he getting his life in order and trying to screw mine up?

"Nah, I'm good." I politely let her down.

"You sure? I'm not looking for anything serious, just a night of fun." She licks her luscious, red painted lips while eyeing me.

Not gonna lie – I'm tempted. She's gorgeous. And I'm pre-tipsy. And horny – it's been a while.

And my ego is a bit bruised by Rae brushing me off earlier tonight when I called her.

"Yeah, I'm sure. Hope you're still able to have a night of fun." I turn and leave, not giving her a chance to try to persuade me.

In my truck, I contemplate swinging by Rae's place. I miss her.

Saint words from earlier come back to haunt me. *Can you marry Rae knowing she doesn't want to have children?*

My cellphone vibrates in my pocket, I pull it out.

"Malik." Her voice is pleasant.

"Hey."

"I miss you."

"Hmmm."

"Can you...can you come over? We should talk."

"O...okay. I'll be there in fifteen."

"I can't wait. I miss you."

***

Sometime later, I park my truck in front of Drew's garage. It's late, but I'm hoping Drew and or Deirdre are awake. I need advice. After leaving her house, I'm more confused than ever. I use my key and let myself inside my brother's house. I quickly disengage, then reset the alarm.

Hearing someone in the kitchen, I walk in that direction.

"You're lucky I saw you on the security camera. You're only supposed to use that key in case of emergency. You don't sleep here anymore."

I take a seat on the stool at the kitchen island. "Sorry. But I really need to talk. Where's Drew?"

"Your brother is knocked out. Kason's baseball team wore him out today. And I helped put him to sleep some time ago." She wiggles her eyebrows. I want to vomit. Deidre is my sister-in-law, but she feels more like a blood sister and the thought of her and my brother – I just can't.

"Spare me the details."

Deidre looks over her shoulder at me. "What's up? You look like something heavy is bothering you."

"Rae doesn't want to have children." I give her a quick rundown of the situation.

Deidre silently wipes the counter after loading the dishwasher. It takes her maybe a full minute before she responds. "Malik, no woman would go through five pregnancies and miscarriages if she didn't want children." She sighs. "You want to know why Kason is the only child?"

"Because you and Drew only wanted one?"

Deidre shakes her head. "Drew and I kept it hush because it was too painful to talk about. But it took me three years to get pregnant after I had Kason and when I did, I had a miscarriage two months into the pregnancy." She's staring off in space like she's reliving the moment.

I'm shocked that I'm just hearing this information.

"It was devastating. The cramping, the pain, then the blood...it's the worst thing I have experienced in my life. I grieved the loss privately for a long time and I vowed never to put myself through that again.

God blessed us with Kason and we were content with that. Rae lost all her babies, Malik. Why would you think she would be okay with risking the chance of another loss?"

I feel like an insensitive a-hole. I have been projecting my desire for children over Rae's terrible losses. After all she's been through, it's not unreasonable that Rae would be afraid of experiencing losing a child again – whether through natural conception, surrogacy or adoption.

"I'm an idiot." I say out loud. "And I did something stupid tonight." I shake my head. "Janae."

Deidre shoots daggers at me with her eyes. "You didn't."

I bow my head in shame. "Yeah. Cause of Saint and his dumb advice."

"You are an idiot! Anything regarding Janae is an asinine mistake. Saint ain't all the way gave his life to Christ so why would you take advice from him?"

"This whole kid issue with Rae messed with my head and then I called her this evening and she acts like she wants nothing to do with me."

"I'm almost positive your fiancée is at home probably heartbroken over the fact that she can't give you what you want, what she wants – children."

I'm such a fool!

"What advice did Saint give you?"

I tell her.

"Are you out of your mutha –" Deidre clamps her mouth shut. I would laugh if the situation wasn't serious and about my stupidity. "Malik, if you weren't my brother-in-law, I would slap that beard right off your face. Saint's advice is stupid as hell. And if you're gonna follow it – Janae for sure is the worst choice."

"I know."

"Then why, Malik? Rae is your good thang. Your fiancée. Her not able to have children shouldn't disqualify her of that – of your love and respect. Damn!"

"I know."

"Did you sleep with Janae?"

"No."

Deidre sighs audibly.

"Answering her call and going over to her apartment was a huge mistake. I was only there for ten minutes. She apologized for how she treated me during and after our break-up. She indicated that she wanted us to give our relationship a try again. I told her I'm engaged, and I'm in love with my fiancée. I left afterwards."

"You finally got that girl off your scent and you answer her call and go over to her house? Are you ready for her crazy again? Because you showing up there in the middle of the night, despite the fact that you told her you're engaged and in love with Rae showed that there's weakness in your relationship. Women like Janae will use that to their advantage."

I shake my head, unconvinced. "Janae knows that what we had is over and never happening again. I love Rae."

"Well start acting like you love Rae. Drew would be building a doghouse if he did something stupid like that to me. You shouldn't have gone over to her house, period. But I understand you are in a vulnerable place and had a moment of weakness. Hopefully Rae gives you a pass."

"You think I should tell her?"

"You better. Because Rae hearing it from Janae will be a lot worse."

"Janae isn't in the picture."

"Trust me – you going over to her apartment placed her in the frame."

17

RAE

I feel terrible for how I reacted to Malik calling me last night. He must think I'm a bipolar, capital B-word. But I couldn't help how short I was with him when he called. Malik wanting kids and my inability to make that happen has me feeling defensive, terrified, worthless and I'm experiencing PTSD.

Greg.

I'm afraid of a repeat of what I experienced with my ex-husband. I never should have agreed to dating Malik which led to us falling in love and now we're engaged with a destination wedding planned in a few months. I knew this would happen, but I went with my heart instead of my head.

I have to break off the engagement.

Just the thought has my heart breaking into smithereens.

I love him!

"Rae, can you answer that pharmacy call?" Yasmine calls over her shoulder. She's at the register ringing up a customer.

I was so deep in my thoughts I didn't hear the phone ringing until now. "Pharmacist Rae speaking, how can I help you?"

For the next few hours, Yasmine and I work our shift without any hiccups.

When I step out of the building heading towards my car, I notice Malik's handsome physique right away, leaning against the hood of his truck parked next to my car. My heart skips a beat. I'm so in love with this man.

"We need to talk," Malik says right away and in a tone that leaves me no room for argument.

"Okay."

"I'll follow you home." Malik goes to stand near the driver's door to my car, waiting for me to unlock it and come closer.

I hit the key fob, unlocking the door which he opens for me. After the way I treated him on the phone last night, he's still being a gentleman. Standing close to him, I get a whiff of his cologne with a hint of freshly cut grass and sweat - and it smells too good. I ache for him to hug me close for his scent to cling to me. He doesn't though.

I get in my car. Malik closes the door then goes and gets in his truck. The whole drive to my house, I'm trying to keep myself together as I come up with the right words to end the best relationship of my life.

I think I'm on the verge of a panic attack. My heart is beating rapidly, and my breathing is getting shallow. *"For God has not given us a spirit of fear, but of power and of love and of a sound mind." 2 Timothy 1:7*. The Scripture helps calm my nerves as I unlock the door to my house. I can feel the heat of Malik behind me. His silence makes what I know I must do even more difficult.

Inside my condo, I place my purse and keys on the side table near the door. I hear Malik shut the door behind me. I turn to face him.

"We have to break up!"

"I love you!"

Malik and I spoke at the same time. His eyes round in shock and my heart disintegrates.

"What? Why?" Malik steps closer to me while I step back. As much as I wanted to hug him earlier, there's no way I will stand firm on my decision if he touches me.

"I can't give you children. And if I even wanted to take the chance on getting pregnant again, I'm forty which means my chances of pregnancy has decreased. Which also increases the pregnancy risks at my age. A woman your age would be more suitable—"

"Rae, I love you. I don't want anyone else."

"But you want children, Malik, and I can't give them to you. And years from now, I don't want to see resentment in your eyes because you chose me over what you really want. A wife you love who also gives you children."

Malik blinks rapidly before shutting his eyes briefly. I know he's wrestling with his emotions like I am. Yes, we love each other, but that doesn't mean we're meant for forever. We have to go our separate ways. *Lord help me!*

"But I love you, Rae. Yes, I want children, but I want you more." He moves closer to me and I step back more into the living room.

I shake my head. "You say that now. A year or more from now, it could be much different." And I know firsthand what much different looks like.

"No, I won't." He moves closer to me and I step back bumping into the couch. "I did something stupid last night. I... I went over to Janae's apartment thinking...maybe –"

"Maybe she can have your baby?" My heart is already destroyed by telling him we need to end us. But knowing he went to another woman still burns me to the core. And it proves my point – painfully so.

"Yes, but...she's already pregnant..."

My head spins.

"...I'm not the father, Rae..."

I mentally and physically blow a sigh of relief.

"...I was upset about how dismissive you were with me yesterday, and yes I have been stressing over the issue of us having children. I had a few beers and had a lapse in judgement. But I was only at her place for ten minutes. She apologized about how she'd been acting before and after our breakup and she did ask for another chance. But standing at the threshold of her apartment, I realized even more so how large my love is for you. I can't see myself with anyone but you, Rae. I. Want. You!"

Tears blind my eyes. My heart and head are at war.

Malik reaches to touch me, but I shake my head. "Baby, please. We will work through this."

"I can't." I swallow my sob. "I love you too much to let you give up on having children. I have already lived that life with Greg. It will kill me if I have a repeat with you."

"I'm not Greg. Please don't do this. Rae, I love you. Please don't do this." Malik gathers me into his comforting arms.

I cry. Hard. Blubberingly so.

"God, I love you so much, Rae. We will figure this out together."

I push out of his arms and step out of his reach. The sorrow in Malik's eyes will stay with me forever. I find strength from somewhere to do what I need to do. "We're done. I don't want children." I swallow the lie. "Please, just leave. Leave!" I scream in hope to get him out of here quicker.

Malik watches me. A barrage of emotions skitters across his face. Then without uttering a word, he leaves me to grieve.

18

RAE

"Get your butt up!" Yasmine snaps on me. Besides Malik, she's the only other person with a key to my condo for emergency purposes. I guess this is an emergency.

I peer from under the covers to see her round belly pointing right at me.

"Get up, Rae! You've called out from work for three days. You've not been answering my calls and texts. I figured you had some personal things to deal with and needed space. Well guess what heifer, time's up. Now sit up and tell me what's going on because I'm not going to have you stressing out my son in my womb because I'm worried about you."

That does it. I flip the covers from over me and sit up.

"On second thought, go back under the covers. You look like death."

I fling a pillow at her. She laughs while catching it.

Yasmine climbs into bed next to me. "What's going on?"

I give her the rundown of what happened between Malik and I three days ago.

It hurts. "I broke up with Malik."

"What...why? You two were my couple goals."

"He wants children and I can't give them to him."

"Did he want to break up?"

"No. But I've already experienced a resentful marriage because of my lack of birthing children. I didn't want that to happen to me and Malik."

"Malik isn't Greg. He isn't an insensitive jerk."

"But –"

"But what? You two could have a wonderful marriage without children. A lot of couples don't have children and still love each other. Marriage isn't just about procreating. Look at me, I'm pregnant by a man I'd only known for three hours. I could only hope the Lord blesses me with a man that would love me whole the way Malik loves you."

"You think I made a mistake?"

"Duh! And that engagement ring that's still on your finger should be your answer to that. Let go and let God. It may be a cliché, but it holds a lot of truth. You're still clinging to your past with your ex-husband when God is trying to give you a better future with Malik. And are you gonna leave him available for Janae to snatch him back up?"

Heck no!

Yasmine laughs reading the expression on my face. "I thought so. Now get up. Shower and do something with that bird nest on top of your head.

Then let's go get your man back."

***

MALIK

"Dude, we left Men's Fellowship and you're still giving me the stink eye. Far as I know, I haven't done anything foul to you." I tell Drew.

Drew, Saint, Kason, and I are getting lunch at our usual spot after weekly Saturday Men's Fellowship whenever I can fit it into my business schedule.

"You know why I'm pissed at you." Drew puts down the menu after deciding what he's going to order.

"Nah, bro, I don't."

"Rae Cooper."

My heart skips a painful beat. "What about her?"

The waiter comes interrupting us. We place our food and drink orders.

"You gave up too easily."

Kason and Saint's eyes volley between me and Drew.

I huff a breath, not wanting to talk about it. I've been slowly dying since she told me to leave her place.

"Dad is right, Uncle Malik. You ran after Janae a few times when she was being her *dramatic* self." Kason actually uses air quotes to describe her. "And she wasn't worth all the fuss."

I don't know how to feel about my thirteen-year-old nephew schooling me.

"Exactly. And you so easily let Rae go. She's your person, bro." Drew shakes his head. "I need to stop letting Deidre twist my arm into watching all her chick flicks... Anyway, Rae is worth fighting for. She's who you've been praying for. God delivered, now look at you. Sitting here letting your blessing go."

"I told him." Saint speaks up.

"Nig – you the one that was trying to convince me to get another chick pregnant. Get from out of here." I wave Saint off.

"And you know you can't always take advice from me. I'm not all the way saved yet." Saint takes a swig of his drink.

"Rae doesn't want to marry me. She doesn't want to try to have my children. She thinks I will become like her ex-husband. She ended things –"

"Because she's afraid, idiot! Give her space, but don't give in to her fears. It's been three days, so after lunch, go to her. The fact that she didn't throw her engagement ring in your face makes me believe there's hope for you two to work things out." Drew looks exasperated with me.

Maybe Drew is right.

"Or, you can turn around and talk to Rae now." Saint says looking over my shoulder.

My heart starts pounding in my chest. I turn around to the most beautiful sight. My good thang.

I'm out of my seat in seconds. Rae walks towards me with a bit of uncertainty. Her friend, Yasmine, stands off to the side by the hostess stand.

"I'm sorry, Malik. I love you! I don't want to call off our engagement. I'm afraid, but I know we can figure out our options for kids, together."

I take Rae in my arms and kiss her passionately, forgetting all the patrons in the restaurant. I stay away from kissing her this way because – the whole trying to stay pure until marriage thing – but...

"Damn, bro! Your wedding night is gonna be lit if y'all kissing like that," Saint outbursts, which brings me back to reality.

I release Rae's lips from mine, with my eyes still closed, and catch my breath.

"I love you and I'm never letting you go." I confess to her. I turn to the guys. "Sorry, but I've got to go. My fiancée and I have things to discuss."

They each give me cheesy smiles while waving us off.

Lord, thank you for not allowing me to lose my blessing.

19

MALIK

My life is once again, good. I got my fiancée back. It's been two months since that day in the restaurant. Rae and I have decided to try surrogacy for having children because we both want biological children.

We just left a consultation.

"What do you think?" I reverse out of the parking space.

"Honestly, I am a bit scared of not finding the perfect candidate to carry our child. I've watched enough Lifetime movies about these scenarios to be freaked out."

"Yeah, like that movie with Regina Hall and Morris Chestnut."

"Oh my god! *When the Bough Breaks*. Their surrogate was crazy! I pray we don't experience anything near that."

"God is going to bless us tremendously. We will find the right person to carry our baby." I reach for Rae's hand, bringing it to my lips for a kiss, with my eyes on the road. "We're going to trust and believe in God's favor for our lives."

"Yes! Thank you. I appreciate your ability to lift me up when I'm in doubt. I didn't have this with Greg... I also never apologized for comparing you to him or lashing out on you because of fear of you treating me the way he did. I'm sorry."

I briefly take my eyes off the road to look at her. "I accept your apology. I love you."

"I love you too... Where are we going? You passed our exit."

"I want to show you something. We'll be there in ten minutes."

"Hmmm, okay. So, my parents booked the restaurant for our rehearsal dinner."

"Perfect. Eight weeks until we're in Florida and I make you my wife."

"I can hardly wait. I hope there are no hiccups. And the weather is perfect for our beach vows."

"Babe, it could be a hurricane and it won't stop the show. You gon' be my wife November nineteen!"

She laughs like I'm playing. I was ready to wife her the first time I saw her.

I pull up to my destination.

"You wanted to show me a house being built?" Rae asks.

"Yeah. It's our house being built."

Rae screams. "Malik, babe, are you serious?" She undoes her seatbelt to hug me.

I chuckle at her excitement. I'm also relieved. When she accepted my wedding proposal, I went to work on the plans for purchasing the property and building our house. It's my wedding gift to her. The 2500 square foot rambler with a basement is ninety percent complete. I want Rae to move in right before we're married for her to decorate. I tell her that.

"Thank you, Malik. It's beautiful." Rae has tears in her eyes as we walk up the long, unpaved driveway.

The construction crew is busy finishing up the final details, so we stay out of their way. The yard is 1.5 acres. I will have a portion fenced off for my work trucks and equipment. And maybe build a workshop.

We take a quick tour inside the house. "I want us to decorate together, Malik. I can do the majority if you want. But this is your house too and I want you to like how it looks." Rae hugs me around the waist. We're standing in our unfinished master bedroom.

"Hmmm. I can't wait to undecorate you in here." I nip her on the ear.

Rae giggles. "Me too!" She takes my hand. "But let's leave now before I give in to temptation. You have my love for you bubbling over as it is by surprising me with this house."

"I promise to keep it bubbling over, babe."

20

RAE

Yasmine smirks while watching me inspect the item she had shoved in my hand. "I know you're not blushing." She laughs. "You're not a virgin."

"I'm a born again virgin," I tease.

"Yeah, whatever. You and Malik may be celibate, but you both have experience in the sack. This," she points to the package of edible crotchless panties in my hand, "will be perfect for your honeymoon."

Yeah, I'm definitely getting these.

"I'm nervous." I admit. Abstaining until marriage is one thing – but what if we're not sexually compatible? I place the strawberry and melon flavored undies in my shopping basket. I had accompanied Yasmine to the mall to purchase a few more baby items she needs. Passing by this lingerie store, we decided to stop. My destination wedding is quickly approaching, and I had been meaning to purchase a few things for our big night. Since Malik had showed me our house being built, I had been busy packing to move in before our wedding.

"That he may not like *sushi*?" Yasmine holds up a silk robe she's interested in buying for when she's in the hospital to give birth.

"Oh my gawd, what if he doesn't?"

"Girl, quit tripping." Yasmine gives me a stern look, picking up on my concerns. "Whether he does or not, you and Malik have serious chemistry. He looks at you like he wants to devour you and you give him the same look. You need to be concerned about y'all setting the honeymoon suite on fire with as much pent up passion burning between you two. It's actually quite romantic seeing you two do things the godly way."

"You think so?"

"Yes. And quite frankly, I'm a bit jealous, but in a good way. I'm trusting God for my Boaz too." She rubs her protruding belly with a slight frown on her face.

"Thanks, Yasmine. You'll find your godly man...Are you okay?"

The frown on her face soon turns into a small smile. "I'm fine, just hungry." She continues to rub her belly.

We both purchase a few things before leaving the store. Our next stop is the seafood shack for shrimp and crab legs. Yasmine has been craving them all day.

"I pray Yasir doesn't develop an allergy to seafood from the way I've been eating it." Yasmine briefly runs her hand over her swollen midsection. She looks adorable pregnant.

"Hopefully not –"

"Ahhh!" Yasmine screeches, drawing others and my attention away from cracking open a king crab leg.

I look over and she's clutching her belly with both hands.

"Rae..." her eyes close in agony and I'm out my chair in a flash moving to her side of the table. "My water broke...it's time."

I step in said water reaching her side. I fight my urge to panic and quickly get my mind right to help. I snatch up both our purses on the table. "The hospital is ten minutes away. You think you can walk to the car?"

Yasmine nods. "Yeah. The pain is gone now."

"Okay. We'll time the contractions in the car." I dig in my wallet finding a hundred dollar bill which will cover our meal and tip. I leave it on the table and apologize profusely to the waiter about Yasmine's accident on the floor. He brushes it off and helps get the mother-to-be in the car.

Minutes later, Yasmine is doing her breathing exercises in the passenger seat. I call her doctor via Bluetooth, informing her of the situation.

My best friend is having a baby and I'm so excited for her. I have dealt with my personal losses enough that I'm genuinely happy for Yasmine.

Nine hours later, Yasir is born weighing 8lbs, 2oz and 22 inches long. My heart feels like it will seize in my chest.

And that pesky Negative Nancy voice begins to speak in my mind. *This is her first pregnancy and she gave birth to a healthy child and you had five failed pregnancies.* Then Greg's voice shouts, *You're only half of a woman. You're worthless!*

Tears slip from my eyes as I watch Yasmine nurse her son. Ayaan, her baby's father, is by her side. He looks excited to be a new dad, despite his reluctance to being here for the birth. After a rapid DNA test, it was proven he is the father.

"You good?" Malik asks, encircling my waist from behind. He's here sooner than I thought. He had a landscaping job this morning that I thought would take him longer to complete.

I nod while wiping my tears. "Yeah. I thought you were coming by later."

"I got Saint to cover for me. I missed you last night." Malik kisses my neck. We had plans to see a movie.

"I missed you too." I gesture to Yasmine and the baby. "Isn't he beautiful?"

"From what I can see. Yeah, he is. Our babies will be too."

My heart skips a beat. "Hmmm." Is my noncommittal reply.

I'm reminded of the Scripture Ruth 3:11, *"And now, my daughter, do not fear. I will do for you all that you ask, for all my fellow townsmen know that you are*

a worthy woman."

But fear is a terrifying emotion. *Help me Lord.*

21

MALIK

This cool, clear-sky evening, and the calm blue waters of the Atlantic Ocean as the backdrop to our beachside wedding are absolutely perfect. I'm a few minutes away from making Rae my wife. I anxiously await her arrival as I stand next to the minister, Drew as my best man, and Saint as my other groomsman. Deidre and Yasmine are Rae's bridesmaids. They look nice dressed in matching turquoise, knee-length dresses.

To my surprise and Rae's, Ayaan accompanied Yasmine here to Florida for our big day. He's holding a sleeping Yasir in his arms. Aside from my nephew Kason, they are the only children in attendance.

Saint is cheesing hard at Marley sitting in the front row in front of him. I have a strong feeling I'll be attending their wedding soon.

The song "Everything" by Brian McKnight begins to play. My eyes immediately lock on Rae looking radiant in her wedding dress being escorted to me by her father.

The dam broke.

The love I have for this woman. All the wrong women I dealt with to get to her. The way she just makes everything right by just being her – she makes me want to be the best man I can be. And for the good Lord answering my prayer – I cry.

This day has finally come, and I'm overjoyed.

I feel Drew grip my shoulder. "Momma and daddy are looking down happy that you're getting married to the perfect woman for you."

That makes me cry a little harder. But I quickly wipe my tears with my handkerchief when Rae stands face to face with me. I accept her hand from her father, giving him a quick nod and thank you.

"You are so beautiful," I tell Rae.

"And you are so handsome." She smiles up at me. I guess I'm not too shabby in my tan khaki suit.

Fifteen minutes later, we are husband and wife.

"He who finds a wife finds a good thing, and obtains favor from the LORD." Proverbs 18:22.

"Thank you, Lord!" I shout after I kiss Rae and fist pump the air. Our small group of twenty guests applaud loudly at my outburst.

"This is probably the best day of my entire life," Rae whispers to me as we take our first dance as husband and wife.

Her confession means everything. Especially since that means our wedding and marriage is better than her first. It is my vow to erase every bad memory she's had with Greg.

"Bruh, I gotta tell you something," Saint says, sitting next to me. We were taking a break from the dance floor watching everyone else have fun.

A few seconds pass and he didn't continue.

"What do you have to tell me?"

"I have been attending church with you for the past few months, and your Christian walk of faith has been more profound than anything the pastor has preached about. Marley's faith and conviction too. And Drew, Deidre and Rae. Seeing your faith sold it for me. God is real. And I want to continue living life His way. You are testimony that God blesses those that obey Him. Marley gon' be my wife."

I smile while nodding my head. "That's what's up." I chuckle. "Man, you have come a long way. I'm proud of you manning up. Getting rid of all those chicks and giving your life to Christ." I pat him on the shoulder. "Marley will be a great wife."

Saint smiles. "Yeah."

RAE

I'm married for the second time, but this time feels different. It feels like forever. I'm also anxious for this night to come to a climax – literally. Tonight will be the first time Malik and I become physically intimate.

Will he like what he sees? Will I like what I see? Can he satisfy me sexually? Can I him? We have already discussed our sexual desires during marriage counseling putting us on the same page – but still. What if we don't meet each other's expectations?

I hear the distinctive click of the door lock disengaging to grant us entry. Malik takes my hand to lead me in. Wordlessly, he shuts the door behind me, then presses my back against the wall inside our honeymoon suite.

Malik places his hand on my throat, gently squeezing before his lips descend upon mine, stealing my breath. I kiss him back just as hungrily. He speaks against my moist lips, "Baby, just so you're prepared. We're going to do a whole lot of smashing before we make love."

"Okay," I breathlessly reply. I'm melting with need for my husband and I have a feeling I have no need to worry about whether our wedding night – and beyond – will be satisfying for us both.

I realize more why God intended sex for marriage – it's such an awesome feeling to be physically joined with your person. It heightens our love and solidifies our union.

22

RAE

"Dang, you did not lie. Ayaan went all out for Christmas with the gifts he got Yasir." I shut the door behind me then look around Yasmine's living room. It was a week after Christmas and opened gifts are littered all over the place. All of which are baby items.

Yasmine takes a seat on the couch and I walk over to the playpen in the corner to watch Yasir sleeping on his back.

"Girl! The rest are in Yasir's room. I told Ayaan he needs to keep most of this at his place. My two-bedroom townhome is too small for all this stuff. Yasir will outgrow most of it before he gets time to really enjoy them."

Not able to help myself, I take Yasir out of the playpen and cuddle him in my arms after I quickly washed my hands in the kitchen. Yasmine rolls her eyes at me playfully as I take a seat on the couch. "What? I'm here to babysit so I will deal with his crankiness if he wakes up."

"Between you, my mom and Ayaan, my baby will be spoiled rotten."

"But he's too cute. He has me wrapped around his pinky." Yasir nestles against my chest and my heart smiles, pushing away some of the pain. Holding him is always a bit bittersweet.

"You're right. He's adorable." Yasmine beams with pride.

"So, Ayaan has really been stepping up as a good dad. Does that mean that you two…" I trail off, eager for her to fill me in.

"Are good at co-parenting. Don't forget he tried to clown me when I told him I was pregnant, and he was MIA during my pregnancy. I'm happy he's taken responsibility since Yasir was born. And these past three months, I've gotten to actually know him and he's a nice guy. Thank God! It's crazy how I slept with him after having only met him a few hours before. He finally told his parents about me and Yasir. They ripped him a knew one and he's gonna be in the doghouse with his family for a while.

"But Ayaan and I come from completely different backgrounds. He's Indian and practices Hinduism. I'm bi-racial – half black and half white, and practice Christianity. Me and him won't work. We at least both agreed that we won't pressure Yasir into either religion. When he's older, we will let him decide."

"That's fair…has Ayaan showed interest in you two dating?"

"Ugh! Rae. Just because you're happily married and still in honeymoon phase doesn't mean everyone around you needs to be lovey-dovey too."

"Yeah, but you didn't answer my question."

"Yes, he's showing interest, but I shut it down quick."

"Why?"

"We're unequally yoked. My faith is a deal breaker. Even though I hadn't been strong in my Christian faith before – I am now. It would only cause conflict."

"What if he converts to Christianity?"

Yasmine shakes her head. "That is an H. E. double L no! He's just as rooted in his faith as I am in mine."

"Jeremiah twenty-four verse seven says, 'I will give them a heart to know me, that I am the Lord. They will be my people, and I will be their God, for they will return to me with all their heart.' Only God can change his heart. And God can do so through you."

"Yeah, maybe. But for now, we're good at co-parenting."

"Hmm. Okay. It's time for you to make your hair appointment."

Yasmine stands and stretches. "Thanks for babysitting. And if you don't mind, I want to get my nails done after my hair appointment."

"That's cool. You need a mommy break. Take your time." I assure her. My time with Yasir is precious to me. Being his godmother maybe the closest I will ever come to being a mom.

23

MALIK

"You cut grass?" He chuckles. "She divorced me to marry you. How much do they pay you an hour?" Greg asks.

Saint and I are doing our routine lawncare at Judea's Bakery. This clown just pulled up and noticed me using the weed eater to trim around the cherry blossom tree.

I continue what I'm doing, ignoring the fool, but Saint cuts the power to his weed eater to see what's up.

"You don't hear me talking to you?" Greg asks me. He must have grown himself a new pair of balls since the last time I saw him.

"My man, you need to move on," Saint tells him.

Greg must really be feeling himself today. "What, you're his mouthpiece?"

Greg don't know that Saint is new in his walk with Christ. It would take nothing for him to shove the weed eater down Greg's throat then pray for God's forgiveness after.

"Nah, but this weed eater 'bout to be yours." Saint says. "He doesn't work by the hour when he owns the company. Unlike you, slaving for the gov'ment. Now, move on!"

Greg mean mugs us both. I could not care less. He takes the hint and walks away to enter the bakery.

"Goofy looking dude." Saint laughs. "The good Lord rescued Rae from him fo' sure."

Hearing my bride's name makes me smile. "He sure did."

***

I love being married. I don't know why some people – especially men, run away from the idea of marriage, because I'm enjoying every second of it. Being united as one with the person God has for you is something every living soul should experience. God placed the need for love and companionship in us for a reason. Why not have it in the sanctity of marriage?

I love coming home to my wife. Rae did an amazing job decorating the place, incorporating both of our likes. Our home feels like us.

This evening, I'm home before Rae. She has another hour of work at the pharmacy, so I get dinner ready for her arrival. I fry up some chicken with yellow rice and vegetables. Everything is ready by the time I hear the garage door opening.

"Hey babe," Rae greets me entering the kitchen. She walks over to where I'm standing at the sink and gives me a kiss.

"Hey. How was work?"

"Same old, same old." She looks at our plates prepared on the kitchen island. "Thanks for cooking dinner. Give me a sec to kick off my shoes and get a little comfortable."

Moments later she's back in the kitchen, looking a bit more comfortable. Rae starts to turn up her nose when I place her plate of food in front of her at the kitchen table. "I don't know what it is, but the smell of chicken is making me nauseous all of a sudden." She pushes the plate away.

I watch as her eyes grow wide in shock. "I...I can't be." She closes them as if she's in pain.

"What? You can't be what?"

"Pregnant." Rae stares at me in fear.

But I'm too happy to pay much attention to it. She's a woman and knows her body. If she thinks she's pregnant, she's pregnant. And, oh man! "We're having a baby!"

I jump up from the table, fist pumping the air. Then I go to Rae's side to help her up. "If you're feeling nauseous go lay down. I will bring your plate up minus the chicken. Then I'm going to purchase a pregnancy test so we know for sure."

Rae remains mute as I help her upstairs to our bedroom. I return later with three pregnancy tests.

"You need me to help you with anything?" I ask, watching Rae lay out all three tests on the bathroom counter. It's like she's physically here with me, but emotionally somewhere else. But again, at this moment, I'm too excited about confirming her pregnancy to press the issue.

"No. I will pee in the cup and place all three sticks inside to confirm or deny."

A few anxious moments later, all three tests confirm we're having a baby. I'm convinced Rae got pregnant on our wedding night six weeks ago.

Rae cries uncontrollably which finally knocks some sense into me. She's afraid of losing our baby.

24

RAE

I want to die.

I literally want to die!

Malik and I got home an hour ago from my doctor's appointment to officially confirm my pregnancy. I'm six weeks along. Our baby's heartbeat is strong and he or she looked like a perfect peanut on the ultrasound monitor.

But I know all too well how soon that all will change.

I won't survive another miscarriage. I won't. I had finally come to terms with all my losses. Now this…

I had assured Malik that I was okay before he left for his job appointment. I lied. Of course, I did. Lord help me, my husband is overjoyed with thoughts of becoming a father. And I'm curled up in our bed in a fetal position knowing that in a matter of days or short weeks, my pregnancy will come to a tragic end like all the others before.

How can I hope for something that has repeatedly been taken away from me? I never should have married Malik. I never should have had an ounce of faith in the impossible.

I never should have missed my appointment for semi-permanent birth control right before our wedding. Darn my feeble heart for hoping I could possibly give my husband children from my womb. I accidently did this on purpose, hoping, now look at me.

Sobs rack my body.

Your body is only good enough for sex, and that's been trash lately. I hate hearing Greg in my head, but times like this conjure up too many painful memories.

"Rae?" I hear Deidre calling my name from downstairs. I bet Malik told her to come over to check on me. We gave her and Drew a spare key.

I'm too weak and distraught to even try to hide my pain. Everyone will be grieving with me soon enough as history repeats itself.

I don't bother calling out to her. She'll find me.

"Rae," Deidre whispers, discovering me on my bed. "Oh honey, God will not fail you."

He already has. I quickly repent of the thought.

I feel Deidre sit on the bed. Her hand lays on my arm. "When I had my miscarriage, I wanted to die right along with my baby. I know you probably experienced the same. And though my experience doesn't compare to yours, you have to know that the Lord cares. Try in some way to find joy in this pregnancy. You are carrying life in your womb. That's a blessing in itself."

It's hard to respond with the frogs lodged in my throat.

"You are that child's mother and however long the Lord has them with you, you are to nurture and love that baby. Do not check out on your child, on your husband and most importantly, yourself."

I nod in agreement.

But my broken heart. "I don't know if I can...I don't know how," I cry.

"Pray, Rae...Lord, we come before You, asking for Your grace and peace. Heal my sister-in-law's broken heart, Lord. See her through her pain. I pray that she releases her fear to completely trust in You. Help her to see the blessing in the miracle she has growing inside of her. Thank You, Father, for allowing her to be this child's mother. She will love, nurture, and rear him according to Your will. We pray Your will be done, in the precious name of Jesus, amen."

"Amen...Thank you Deidre."

"Any time, Rae. I'm here for you, any time."

25

MALIK

I park my work truck at its designated spot away from the house next to my temporary storage shed. I'm having a permanent work shed with office space above it built in several months.

I cut the engine, but remain in the truck. I look towards our beautifully built home in pride. It's been three weeks since we found out Rae is pregnant and coming home now feels like a game of blackjack. I never know what version of my wife I will get.

I pick up the vase with French tulips and hop out the truck. I find Rae in the family room watching a rerun of Living Single.

"Hey," Rae greets me with a morbid tone.

I place the vase of tulips on the coffee table then lean over to kiss Rae briefly on the lips.

"They are beautiful. Thanks. Dinner is in the oven." She pretty much dismisses me. So today is her pushing me away day. Yesterday was emotional breakdown day filled with tears. The day before that was celebration day because she made it to another week of pregnancy without any signs of loss.

I have been trying my hardest to deal with it all – Rae's pregnancy hormones and fear of losing our baby and me being torn between wanting to be joyous every day because of the life we created in her womb – but watching Rae go through her many emotions made it difficult to enjoy her pregnancy.

It shouldn't be this hard. I feel selfish sometimes because I want her to just get over her fears and enjoy the moment with me. But then knowing all she has endured before me – I understand why she's struggling.

I don't want her to lose our baby either, but I also don't want to have that thought as the highlight of our lives for the next few months.

"For God has not given us a spirit of fear, but of power and of love and of a sound mind." I have been quoting second Timothy one verse seven daily for both Rae and me.

I sit next to Rae on the couch instead of leaving like she would prefer. "We are two months into our marriage. You are pregnant with our child, so I refuse to give in to you disregarding me whenever you feel like it. I understand you are dealing with pregnancy hormones and sometimes you can't help your up and down moments, but pushing me away ends now."

Rae continues to watch the television show as if she doesn't hear me. I grab the remote from the coffee table and shut the T.V. off.

"I was watching that!"

"And I'm trying to have a conversation with my wife. This is exactly what I'm talking about. You're ignoring me."

"I don't feel like talking."

"Fine. Listen. Help me help us. The cycle we've been going through for the past few weeks isn't working. I know you're terrified of possibly losing our baby..."

Tears pool in Rae's eyes, but I don't let them distract me.

"...But living in that constant fear isn't healthy for you. Both emotionally and physically. Release your fears to God, Rae. Quote second Timothy one verse seven every time you feel anxious and afraid. Don't allow the enemy to hold you hostage to the past. Now is supposed to be one of the best times of marriage. Please let us enjoy every second of it – together."

Rae brushes the tears from her face. "I know. I'm sorry. I try so hard most days. I really, really try not to let fear overtake me. But the memories are so vivid. So painful. I want our baby more than anything in this world."

I gather Rae in my arms, hugging her to me. "I know you do, babe. I want our baby more than anything, too. I'm not expecting you to instantly overcome your fear, but please don't push me away. I love you. We're in this together."

"I love you too, so much. You make this whole experience bearable. Forgive me for being a B-word earlier. I don't mean it. My hormones are out of whack, but it's still no excuse."

I chuckle as she tickles my side, bringing a much welcomed end to our conversation.

"My hormones and I want to properly apologize for our behavior." Rae nibbles on my ear.

This is one pregnancy effect that I do enjoy, though we can't do much with Rae's pregnancy being high-risk because of her previous miscarriages. Rae is also afraid of hurting our baby during sex, so we are improvising.

Her doctor has been closely monitoring her pregnancy, so far everything is progressing well. I pray to God it remains that way.

26

MALIK

"No way!" Rae and I say in unison.

We are at Rae's 16-week prenatal appointment. The past weeks have been a roller coaster ride of emotions for both of us. Mostly Rae. There were a few times I thought I would have to get her checked out for depression. She was scaring the crap out of me because of her fear of miscarriage.

But she made it to four months pregnant and we celebrated big this past weekend with family and friends. This is the longest Rae has carried any baby. Every day since we found out she's pregnant, I have been placing my hands on Rae's belly and praying for our baby.

Rae will continue to have a healthy pregnancy and she will deliver our healthy child. All will be well with my wife and kid.

Well – wife and children.

"Triplets?" I have never been more shocked in my life.

Rae bursts into tears.

"Babe, it's okay." I reassure her.

"I know. I'm crying because I'm happy. God is blessing us with three babies."

"Instead of shame and dishonor, you will enjoy a double share of honor. You will possess a double portion of prosperity in your land, and everlasting joy will be yours." Isaiah 61:7.

"You have been measuring big so I had a feeling there may be more than one in there. Those two were hiding well during the last few ultrasounds. This is a tremendous blessing you two. Congratulations," Dr. Pauline says. "And I must say, in all my years, you're my first patient pregnant with triplets. Rae, your pregnancy is progressing well. Rest assured, with triplets you may deliver a little before the forty-week mark, but that's normal."

"Thank you!" Rae is smiling from ear to ear now.

"Do you want to know the sex of the babies?" Dr. Pauline asks.

"Yes!" Both Rae and I say together.

"Okay, let's see...Baby A is...a boy...Now let's see if baby B will cooperate...Ah, another boy...Okay three's a charm. What is baby C...a girl!"

I feel like I'm about to pass out – cold. My heart is overpowered with joy. Two sons and a daughter. *Thank you, Lord.*

"Aww, mommy's babies." Rae reaches her arm to touch the monitor. "I love you guys so much. Can we get a few copies of the ultrasound?"

"Yes, of course." Dr. Pauline prints them out, then cleans up the solution on Rae's belly from performing the ultrasound.

Rae and I leave the doctor's office grinning like Cheshire cats. I think we float to the car.

"When do you want to tell everyone?" I ask Rae while starting the engine.

"I don't. Won't it be more fascinating for our family and friends to find out the day of delivery?"

"Whoa. You seriously don't want to tell anyone? Babe, I don't know if I can hold it in. I'm too excited."

Rae reaches for my free hand while I drive. "I know. With all I've been through, I want to shout it to the world. But I also want to have this moment for myself for a while. I'm also a little nervous about carrying multiples, but I want to enjoy each moment having them inside me. And it will be a pleasant surprise for everyone when our children arrive."

"Actually, your plan is cool. They will get the shock of their lives, like we just did."

"Yup. So, we're both going to promise to keep it to ourselves?"

"Yeah, let's do it."

27

RAE

"Rae, are you sure you're not carrying twins?" Yasmine asks, watching me waddle to my comfy seat to start my day. At six months, pregnant I reduced my hours in the pharmacy. I come in three days a week for six hours. Malik thinks I should take time off now until the babies come. But I already know it would be months before I'm behind a pharmacy counter when the triplets arrive. I have no interest coming back full time after giving birth, but I won't quit my profession. When I return to work, at least six months postpartum, my hours will remain like they are now.

"Is that your polite way of saying I look like an elephant?"

"Well…"

"Really, Yasmine? I never once said you looked like a whale when you were pregnant with Yasir," I joke.

"Unlike you, I have trouble filtering my thoughts. But thank you for not calling me Shamu."

I stick my tongue out at her. "And yes, I'm positive I'm not pregnant with twins."

"Coulda fooled me. Despite how round you are at six months, you are cute or whatever."

"Yasmine, is this attitude because you are you still salty that I cut my hours? It's been three weeks."

"Because you and I had a good thing going for a long time, then you just had to let Malik get you pregnant. And even though you, Malik, and apparently your doctor are delusional with the fact that you definitely have more than one bun in the oven, you cut your hours and have me making up the time with Brenda."

I stifle a laugh. I know she is only lashing out because she misses working all her hours with her bestie. And Brenda is a fifty-five year old pharmacist that acts like she was born in the Ice Age. Brenda's brand of boredom is better than the sleeping pill, Ambien.

"Yet you waste our precious time together fussing at me. Besides, Brenda is relocating to Texas in a month and hopefully the new pharmacist won't be a bore."

"They better not be. Because according to you, after the *twinssss* arrive, you won't be back here for half a year."

"From what I've heard, the new prospect is in his early forties, like me, married with a son and daughter. He's a pharmacist by day and drag queen at night. I think you will like him."

"Well, I did always want a gay best friend."

"Oh no, I said nothing about you two being best friends. That's my status in your life."

"Aww, don't be jealous. If anything, he'll only be my work bestie. You will be my all the time bestie."

"Fine! And for the record, I'm not pregnant with twins."

"Denial is not a good look on you." Yasmine buttons her pharmacy coat.

"I'm not. Turn around, there's a customer approaching."

"Good morning, are you dropping off or picking up?" Yasmine asks the two gentlemen that approached the counter together.

"We are here to speak with Rae Cooper...er...Rae Day. Is she available?"

"And who may I say is here to see her?"

I can see and hear the exchange and my hackles go up. But I remain quiet, letting Yasmine do her thing.

"I'm Preston Daniels."

"And I'm Derek Burrows. We're attorneys at Adderley Law Group in DC."

I manage to get down from my comfy highchair to approach the counter. "I'm Mrs. Day. What do you need to speak with me about?"

"It's regarding our client and her lawsuit against your ex-husband."

Go figure. I divorced the man and still have to deal with his nonsense. "Okay, go over to that door I'll meet you there." I pointed the door out to them.

I let them into the breakroom. "What is all of this about?"

Preston replies, "Our client, Tania Dean, filed a lawsuit against Greg Cooper accusing him of putting drugs in her food to cause her to miscarry their child."

It's like the wind got knocked out of me. I feel faint...

"Mrs. Day are you all right?" Derek asks catching me by my arms and helping me to sit at the table in the small room.

"Yes. Pregnancy symptom. Can you please get me a glass of water?" I point to the water dispenser near the fridge.

"Yes, sure."

I gladly take the cup of water, drinking it slowly. Both men watch me to make sure that I'm indeed well.

"Please forgive us if we have upset you," Preston says.

"It's okay."

Hell no, it's not okay. That bastard he… he… could he? Did he?

"We wanted to know if you may have experienced or suspected anything similar when you were married to Mr. Cooper."

I can't do this. My babies… all five…

"Can you please call my husband? Please. I won't be able to handle the rest of this conversation without him."

"Yes, of course. How can we contact him?"

MALIK

Biggie... or Notorious B. I. G.'s lyrics from the song "Who Shot Ya?" is on heavy rotation in my mind. Lord knows I should probably be quoting Scriptures, but I've been on ten since the attorney called me to meet at the pharmacy with Rae.

My wife has been upset all day to the point I had to take her for an emergency check up with Dr. Pauline just to make sure her and the babies are all right.

Rae and the babies are well physically – but my bride is an emotional wreck. She finally settled down and went to sleep an hour ago. I called Yasmine to come and stay with her because I needed to get away for a bit, not before taking my licensed Glock out the safe. I need someone to talk me out of pulling the trigger on that nigga.

That bastard caused Rae to lose all her babies and blamed her for not being able to bring life into the world.

"That grimy muthafu –" Psalm 19:14 shuts me up quick. *"Let the words of my mouth and the meditation of my heart be acceptable in your sight, O Lord, my rock and my redeemer."* "Lord, I don't want to think or speak holy! Greg did my wife dirty."

"Aww bro, the first sign of being crazy is when you start talking to yourself," Drew says, watching me approach the garage where he stood checking the oil in Deidre's car.

"I'm talking to God. Between you and Him, one of y'all need to stop me from wanting to blow Greg's brains out."

"Whoa! Rae's ex? What did he do?"

I give Drew a quick rundown.

"Word?" He shakes his head. "I'm sorry, bro. That is messed up."

"Exactly. Now give me a reason not to hunt him down and give him a slow painful death."

"Rae and your unborn child." Drew slams the hood down to Deidre's car.

That helps, but... "If you were in my shoes, would you just let it slide?"

"If I were in your shoes, I would probably need you to talk me out of killing him if I hadn't done it already... I know it's hard sometimes living up to our Christian values, especially when dudes like Greg need some street justice – but bro, he ain't worth it. He will win at hurting Rae all over again because you may feel some vindication for ending him – but you will lose everything in return. And Rae would have to grieve her husband going to jail for life."

"Thanks Drew, that's exactly what I needed to hear." I look up to the evening sky, sending a silent thank you to God for leading me to Drew instead of the alternative. Saint would have helped me kill Greg and get rid of the body.

28

RAE

I'm not worthless. I'm not a pathetic case of a woman. I'm not incapable of carrying a child in my womb for more than three months. My body isn't only good enough for sex. I will birth my children. I will become a mother…

Once and for all, I'm erasing every lie Greg spoke over my life.

"Don't forget your lunch," I call out to Malik, picking up his lunch cooler that I filled with two sandwiches that would rival a Panera sandwich for him and Saint, fruit salad, chips, water and Gatorade. I walk to the kitchen door leading to the backyard to hand it to him.

"Thanks babe, Saint would have my head if I forgot your homemade lunch."

"Saint is just greedy. But I'm glad he enjoys them."

"I do too...Don't forget to email the potential clients those estimates for me later."

I peck Malik's lips. "Of course. Have a good day at work."

Returning to the kitchen island, I slide my Bible in front of me and flip the pages to Isaiah 53:4-5. "Surely He took up our pain and bore our suffering, yet we considered Him punished by God, stricken by Him, and afflicted. But He was pierced for our transgressions, He was crushed for our iniquities; the punishment that brought us peace was on Him, and by His wounds we are healed."

I meditate on the Scripture and what it means in relation to me receiving once and for all my complete healing and deliverance from the poison I allowed Greg to sicken me with.

I am healed in Jesus's name.

Two weeks since the lawyers showed up at my job – I had to grieve my losses all over again – for new reasons. I'm putting it behind me now. Greg will get all that is due to him for the pain he inflicted on me and his ex-girlfriend, Tania Dean.

Greg allegedly did what he did to Tania (and me) because he already has five children. Five! All of which he had before he married me. I had absolutely no clue whatsoever. Apparently, his high school sweetheart who he has the kids with, moved to Canada two years before Greg and I started dating. Which may explain why I never met her or the kids. Also, Greg's child support is astronomical. No wonder he wanted more than his share from the sale of our house.

I almost wanted to be pissed with Greg for keeping such a secret from me for the entirety of our relationship – but I'm more relieved. Relieved that I am no longer tied to him.

My heart breaks for what Tania endured. Losing a child is one of the worst experiences of life. But I hope that, like me, she will again get pregnant and have a healthy pregnancy, birth, and raise beautiful children.

I told the lawyers everything they wanted to know and I'm sure my experience and Tania's is a strong case against Greg. I'm sure of one thing – Greg is a psychopath. He deliberately caused the death of unborn children.

29

MALIK

"Yes!"

Everyone still standing around in the church lobby after the last service for the day applaud at Marley accepting Saint's marriage proposal.

The newly engaged couple embrace in a hug. Rae is taking pictures of them on her cellphone, along with a few other people.

I smile wide. My boy is all grown up. To see Saint evolve in his Christian faith is a miraculous thing. I'm proud of the man he is and I'm thankful to God to saving us – all of us.

"Congratulations, Marley and Saint." I hug Marley then Saint. I knew he was going to propose soon – he had the ring for a week. I just didn't know he would do it today after church.

"Thank you, Malik. I'm so happy. I can't wait to call my parents to tell them." Marley says beaming at her groom-to-be. They are a good looking couple and I believe they will have a great marriage and family.

"Soon you will be me, married and pregnant," Rae says to Marley while rubbing her protruding middle. At seven months pregnant, she looks more beautiful to me each day.

"I'm looking forward to it. But according to this guy, I will be pregnant with at least twins for my first pregnancy." Marley playfully pokes Saint in the side.

Saint grins. "Yup. The good Lord and I have an understanding. I want us to have a big family. Marley does too."

"I do. We're thinking four kids," Marley agrees.

"Rae and I want to shoot for three," I say.

Rae looks at me, giving me a knowing look.

"And Rae looks like she's already carrying all three of them," Yasmine walks up beside us, pushing

Yasir in his stroller. She joined Journey to Faith church a few months ago.

"Girl, I told you to stop commenting on my pregnancy weight. My baby has me eating a lot."

Which is true, Rae is always hungry.

"I believe you. I just like to tease." Yasmine turns to the engaged couple while Rae coos at Yasir blowing spit bubbles. "A little birdie in the nursery told me that congratulations are in order?"

Marley gushes while showing Yasmine her diamond ring. "Yes. We're getting married."

Yasmine hugs Marley. "Congratulations! I had a feeling it was coming soon." She then hugs Saint. "You did good man. You proposed to the perfect woman and got her a nice ring."

"Thanks. I feel underserving of it all, but I thank God for His blessings. Marley is one of the best things that has happened to me."

"Wow! I look forward to sharing a love like that with someone one day. Both of you couples are goals."

"Thanks Yasmine. If God did it for us, he will do it for you," Saint says.

"Amen to that, brotha. I receive it in Jesus's name."

30

RAE

"This is bull! Y'all be ripping people off with these prices for medication!" A middle aged, irate, white woman fumes at Yasmine.

I can tell my friend is mentally praying to not blow up in this woman's face. Our profession has no shortage of impolite customers.

"Ma'am, I don't create the prices, so I'm not ripping you off. There is a prescription discount program you can sign up for since you're paying out of pocket."

"Don't ma'am me like I'm some eighty year-old woman. And I wouldn't need no gotdamn discount card if y'all didn't make the prices too high."

Yasmine is clearly exasperated. "Miss, I am trying to be polite. I am not responsible for the cost of your medicine –"

"Let me speak with a pharmacist since you are the lackey," The rude woman looks over Yasmine's shoulder to get my attention. "You!" She points at me. "Are you a pharmacist?" She shakes her head. "Probably not since you're bl…I'd like to speak with a pharmacist."

The two customers behind her gasps loudly at her faux pas.

Jesus, Moses, Abraham, David and Peter – help ya girl out. I pin my mouth shut and climb off my comfy highchair.

"I'm the pharmacist on duty. How can I help you, ma'am?"

Miss Rude eyes enlarge in size by my title or my addressing her as ma'am – it's hard to tell which and frankly I don't care. It would be comical if the situation wasn't so tasteless on her part.

"It is ridiculous for me to have to pay eighty dollars for my medication that I have to pay for every month."

How about laying off smoking and start eating proper foods. But I keep that thought to myself. I know exactly what her medications are for. The smell of nicotine on her breath and clothing greets you like an unwanted hug.

"The best I can do is offer you a one-time store discount of ten percent. And like Yasmine mentioned to you, there's a prescription discount card you can sign up for to help with your medication costs." I plaster a fake but pleasant Academy Award winning smile on my face.

"Maybe I need to go to another pharmacy since you can't do better than that," she threatens.

Go! You will be back when you get their prices.
I'm sure she already knows that though. Most of our customers fill their prescriptions with us because the bigger chain pharmacies are too expensive.

"It is your right to do as you choose, ma'am." Again, I give her my award-winning smile.

"Humph! Well since it's already been filled, I will take it…And what is the information to sign up for the discount program?"

"Yasmine will be happy to assist you with that." I turn and wink at Yasmine, then get back to work filling prescriptions. Yasmine checks the woman out along with the two other customers in line.

"We can't go two days without someone fussing over the cost of their medicine." Yasmine turns to look at me. She begins the task of bagging and labeling filled prescriptions.

"Well, it brings some variety to our day." We work in silence for a while.

The hairs on my arm raise. I look up from my task of putting information into the computer to see Greg walking towards the pharmacy counter.

"Na, boo, not today, tomorrow or the day after." Yasmine tells Greg.

"Back off chihuahua," my ex-husband barks out.

"Security!" Yasmine shouts.

Why won't this man leave me alone?

I go to the counter to try and calm the situation. I don't need this drama – especially on my job. "What do you want, Greg?"

He eyes me up and down, with his eyes settling on my seven-month pregnant belly. "You're pregnant." He stands there in awe.

I bet he's shocked since he killed all our babies before they had a chance to be born. I don't have any proof – but I know in my bones he did. Everything his ex-girlfriend Tania said about her experience is similar to my situation with him. After digging through his things, Tania had found a receipt for prescriptions he purchased during a trip he took to Toronto. All the combination of drugs she listed can be used to bring on a miscarriage or abortion. I had a lot of pharmacy books at home that I'm sure he used to look up drugs that can do just that.

Greg is a certifiable psychopath.

Because what he did is more than his desire not to have any more children. If that were the case, he should have gotten a vasectomy. I had continually gotten pregnant because he had expressed how much he wanted children as much as I did. Did he get some evil satisfaction from watching me suffer?

"What seems to be the problem?" Nathan, the bulky security guard on duty asks.

"He's here harassing Rae," Yasmine tells him.

"Dude, you have to leave." Nathan advances on Greg. I have a suspicion that Malik tips the security guards to make sure that me and Yasmine are always safe. Not like we have ever had any serious incidents at the pharmacy. Other than irate customers like the woman earlier.

"Yasmine, I apologize for being rude." Greg shocks the heck out of both Yasmine and I. "Rae, please. I just need five minutes to talk to you. It's important." Greg pleads.

Against my better judgement, I agree. Because I have a feeling he will only persist later if I don't. I make sure Nathan stands by the open door of the breakroom while we chat.

"I need a favor." Greg begins. "My ex-girlfriend recently had a miscarriage and for some insane reason, she's accusing me of putting drugs in her food to cause it. But I would never do such a thing. You know how much I wanted us to have children, but you…" He looks at me sitting in the chair at the table while he is standing. His eyes dart to my protruding middle. "You ah...you couldn't." He clears his throat. "Rae, what I'm asking is if you can testify in my favor."

If I didn't know how heartless he was I would almost believe him. Almost believe that he wasn't capable of...murder!

I stand and proceed toward the breakroom door. "No."

"What?"

"No, I will not testify in your favor."

"Do you realize what this is doing to my reputation? I can lose my government job and status. That I can possibly go to jail for this?"

Yes, I am quite aware.

I turn to face him. "And?"

His nostrils flare and evil Greg reappears. "You owe me, Rae! This is the least you can do for me."

I laugh dryly. "Please further amuse me by telling me what it is exactly that I owe you."

"You bitc –"

I all out laugh. "It must have been killing you to pretend for five minutes that you have a heart." *'Cause now I know you have none.*

Nathan steps more into the room. "Times up!" I had told him five minutes before he is to escort Greg out.

Greg changes his tactic. "Look, I'm sorry. All right? I just need this favor from you, and I promise you won't hear from me ever again."

"Let's go!" Nathan snaps at him. Greg starts moving out of the breakroom. Nathan isn't one to mess with.

"I can't because I already promised Tania that I will testify in her favor."

It's like Greg sees red and begins to charge towards me, but Nathan grips him quickly by his necktie dragging him out of the breakroom and all the way out front, then out of the building like a ragdoll. All the while Greg is cussing and fussing, making a scene for the pharmacy staff and customers.

"Good riddance to bad rubbish." Yasmine says when I return to duty.

31

MALIK

"You know I'm always down for whatever, but this is a bad idea." Saint says from the driver's seat of his Mustang. I'm riding shotgun. "You gonna follow Greg home and kill him? You got too much to lose, man."

"Just follow his car!" I grit through my teeth. Greg messed with the wrong one when he approached my wife to testify in his favor.

Saint does what I ask, driving discreetly behind Greg's SUV leaving the parking lot of the government agency building where he works at in Suitland, Maryland. Traffic at 3pm on a Friday afternoon is ridiculous. After two stops to pick up food and dry cleaning, we finally park two houses down from where

Greg pulls into the driveway of a ranch-style house in a decent looking neighborhood.

The whole drive here, I was anxiously thinking of ways to end Greg's life and get away with it.

We drive away, now knowing where he lives. "Park at the post office we passed earlier. We'll walk back to his house."

Saint looks at me from the corner of his eyes. "Man, you can't be serious. That clown is not worth it."

"Let me handle my business! I just need you to make sure I don't end up in jail."

Saint sighs deeply. "A'ight!"

Saint expertly picks the lock to the front door. We barge in to find Greg looking stupid with a mouthful of Chinese food, eating in front of the television in the living room.

"What the hell are you doing in my house?"

"Why were you at my wife's job?"

"She was my wife first and I can talk to her whenever the hell I want to!" He shouts while standing.

Wrong answer!

I think I may have teleported because in no time, I close the fifteen foot distance to be standing in his face. I swing left, catching him in the jaw. "You forfeited that right when you divorced her."

Greg lifts his fist to strike, but I block it with my arm and kick him in his junk. He falls to his knees like a sinner confessing their sins.

"Stay away from my wife!"

"She was my cunt fir –"

I cut Greg off by yanking him to his feet by his collar. I pull out the revolver from my waist, pressing it against his temple. "Now finish what you were about to say." My jaw clenches. The anger I have radiates like waves over my body.

"Shoot his ass!" Saint shouts.

Is he serious?

With wild eyes, I look over at my boy, while still having a tight grip on Greg's collar with the gun pressed to his temple.

Proverbs 29:11 makes itself known in the forefront of my mind. *"Fools vent their anger, but the wise quietly hold it back."*

I shove Greg away from me. He stumbles over the arm of his settee, falling hard on the hardwood floor.

I point the gun at him. "You're lucky you're going to end up in jail for what you did to Rae and God knows how many other women." After making sure the safety is still on, I place the revolver in the holster on my belt, then cover it with my shirt.

Greg mean-mugs me, but he's smart enough to keep his mouth shut. My faith in God and love for my wife and unborn children are the only things keeping him alive. Plus, he's a punk and not much of a fight. He may become someone's girl in prison if he doesn't toughen up.

I give Greg some parting words. "You and I both know you calling the cops about this won't work in your favor in court. You're on security footage at the pharmacy making a scene that can be used against you in your pending case."

I back away, moving towards the front door where Saint is still standing.

When we're inside Saint's car, I ask, "You were supposed to keep me from doing something stupid. Why would you tell me to shoot him?"

Saint starts his car then pulls off. "I knew me telling you to kill him would conflict with your convictions with God." He shrugs his shoulders. "It worked, didn't it?"

I smile. "Yeah, it did. Good looking out."

Saint nods, "I got you....and I didn't want no smoke from your pregnant wife."

We both chuckle.

32

MALIK

Greg was sentenced to twenty years in prison for fetal homicide. Investigation found receipts dating back to when he was married to Rae, of him purchasing mifepristone, misoprostol and methotrexate, among a list of other drugs in Toronto, Canada, that can cause miscarriage or abortion in women if consumed. Seems when dude was visiting his ex and kids in Canada, he was coming up with ways to kill his unborn children in the states.

Tania noted that the vibe she got from Greg completely changed when she told him she was pregnant. It was like he went from Dr. Jekyll to Mr. Hyde instantaneously, to the point where she became anxious around him. They were together at her home when she miscarried. He treated her with so much contempt that at the hospital she didn't want him near her and immediately told the doctor and nurses she suspected he had something do with her losing her baby.

Tania had stated that Greg had brought her take-out for dinner that night and had filled a cup with juice for her to drink while they watched TV in her family room. Within thirty minutes of drinking it she started cramping. Remembering the half-full glass of juice on her coffee table, she had her brother retrieve it from her house to bring to the hospital. Traces of the drugs were detected in the juice and on the cup after tests were done. Greg probably knew that the drugs cannot be detected in a person's blood, but he was too dumb this time to get rid of the evidence. Or as I believe like the bible talks about, what is done in the dark soon comes to light. Tania immediately took legal actions against Greg.

Tania's lawyers asked Rae if she wanted to also pursue a case against Greg for what he did to her – but unlike Tania, who had a security camera in her family room with clears views of the open kitchen, that showed Greg putting something in her drink, Rae had no physical evidence. Only a gut feeling. Also, Rae didn't want the negative energy regarding her losses with Greg to dampen her current pregnancy.

My wife and I are happy.

Greg is the past. And obviously, he will pay for what he did to both Tania and Rae. Dude is a psychopath, no cap!

It has been hard hiding the nursery from our family and friends. Rae and I have been enjoying our time decorating the large bedroom that our babies will share. Three cribs fit nicely in the room. We kept the décor simple with light gray walls and a pastel palette of light green, pale pink, and subtle blue in the furniture, curtains, rug and sheet fabrics.

We are officially ready for our kids to arrive.

Life is great.

"Babe!" Rae shrieks from somewhere in the house.

I'm in the kitchen trying to make her a grilled cheese sandwich. This should be pretty simple – but I've always sucked at making them just right. But I'm trying, nonetheless, for my pregnant bride.

But her scream has me on high alert. I abandon the bread and cheese to find her. Rae is standing in the foyer clutching her belly.

"It's time, Malik." The pain etched on her face lets me know she's indeed in labor.

"Okay. Okay…" I'm at her side in seconds trying to recall everything we learned in Lamaze class, trying my best not to freak out.

I'm quickly finding it's hard not to at this moment. Rae is thirty-seven weeks pregnant with triplets, so we knew this day was fast approaching.

I scoop Rae up in my arms, heading for the garage door through the kitchen.

"Hospital bag," she says with a more relaxed look on her face. The contraction must have passed.

I turn around, still cradling her, and head for the coat closet near the front door where we stored the bag. I place Rae on her feet briefly to put the strap of the bag on my shoulder then pick her back up, heading for the garage again.

"Stove. I smell the pan burning." Rae smiles up at me.

I detour to the stove and allow her to turn the knob to prevent our home from burning down. I start for the garage door – again.

"Car keys, babe. And don't forget to set the alarm." Rae grins.

"How is it that you're the one in labor, but you have everything under control?" I lean in close to peck her lips.

"God knew one of us needed to be clear headed."

As soon as I get Rae buckled into the car, another contraction crashes into her. She cries out in agony as I helplessly reverse out of the garage praying to God that I get us to the hospital safely.

Ironically, Rae's parents are scheduled to fly into to town tomorrow. Next week was supposed to be the big arrival of the triplets. Our babies have other plans. Apparently.

Rae was scheduled to have a Cesarean section – now she likely will give birth vaginally. My head spins watching Dr. Pauline and the nurses prep Rae for childbirth. Clear fluid rushes out of Rae and I give myself a mental pep talk to man the hell up! This is it. We are about to be parents of three.

RAE

I loathe and anticipate the pain from the contractions. I had given up hope that I would ever experience this. The pain of bringing life into the world. The agony of my babies' desires to be set triumphantly free from my womb.

I love it.

I hate it.

Thank you, God!

I reach for Malik's hand, squeezing it like a python's death grip as a contraction radiates through my body. I don't mean to hurt him. The pain is too much to bear and his nearness brings some relief.

The triplets are coming. I'm too far ahead in the labor process to get an epidural to ease the pain. *Lord if I survive this, I will cherish this pain for ever.*

"Okay Rae, I need you to push with all your might as if you are having a bowel movement," Dr. Pauline calls out from between my legs.

I do as she says and moments later baby A is born. Crying with all his little might. Tears burn my eyes as the nurse brings A over for me and Malik to quickly see before taking our firstborn to be examined.

Another contraction. Pain. Push. Baby B needs a tap on his butt before his cries fill the room. Again, we get a brief peek of our second born, because I have one more to deliver.

The labor process is repeated and finally, C emerges. No cries from our third child. But her eyes are wide open as if we disturbed her beauty rest.

Malik leans down kissing me with tears leaking from his eyes. "Thank you, Rae. Thank you for birthing our beautiful children. I love you."

"I love you! Thank you for not giving up on me – on us. On this."

"Never! I will never give up on us." He kisses me again.

***

My parents were able to change their flight for today. Deidre and Drew are at the airport to pick them up. None of our family and friends have met the babies yet. We told them we wanted them to collectively come together.

"I feel so inadequate right now. You have two boobs with three mouths to feed." Malik looked perplexed as he watches me breastfeed our sons Millo and Malachi. He's holding an already fed Rhesa. Already, I can tell that our daughter is the spitting image of her father. And our sons have more of my features. But time will tell. Our triplets average four pounds each and are fully developed. They won't need a stay in the NICU.

This moment is overwhelmingly the greatest day of my life. I'm a mom.

The Lord would not have to bless me with anything else in my life and I would be content. God has given me everything I ever wanted.

"You're not inadequate because it frees you up for diaper duty," I tease.

Malik looks up from the sleeping beauty in his arms and smiles at me. "Yeah, I'm going to have to buy some goggles."

I giggle. Millo treated his dad to pee in the face earlier when Malik changed him.

About an hour later, I'm propped up in bed after a quick nap with all three babies in my arms. Malik just finished taking a picture on his phone when there's a knock on the door.

Our family has arrived. My mom barges in first with Dad, Deidre, Drew, Kason, Yasmine, Saint and Marley in tow. Mom stops short. I watch as her eyes bounce to all three of my babies cradled in my arms.

"Oh my God!" Mom cries with a smile on her face.

Dad looks dumbfounded.

Drew and Deidre look at me and the babies, then Malik who's standing by my side, sporting the proudest grin.

"Bruh, I know you said y'all wanted three kids, but you can't be taking other people's babies from the nursery. You're black – they will lock you up quick!" Saint says breaking the shocked silence in the room.

"I knew it!" Yasmine exclaims. "I knew you were carrying more than one in that huge belly of yours."

"Surprise!" I belatedly reply.

Everyone congratulates us, coming closer to the bed to see our triplets. Malik is like a guard dog. He makes everyone wash their hands for twenty seconds before they can hold the babies.

Later, when everyone left. Malik and I say our nightly prayer together, ending it with Jeremiah 29:11 "For I know the plans I have for you," declares the Lord, "plans to prosper you and not to harm you, plans to give you hope and a future."

A message from the author:

Thank you for reading and making it to the end! That means you liked it, right? I ask one favor of you if you connected in any way with the characters– if you laughed, cried, if they broke your heart, or you cheered them on– *please leave a review*. I would appreciate it, greatly. Reviews are beneficial for authors to not only improve our craft and learn your likes and dislikes as a reader, it helps us connect with you. Take a few short minutes and leave a constructive review for me. Thanks!

Read you later! (Corny, I know. I couldn't help myself :-))

Let's connect on Instagram: @introvertedkhara

Check out other titles by me if you haven't already…

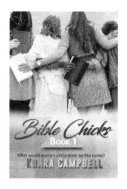 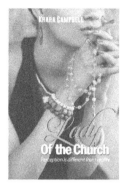

 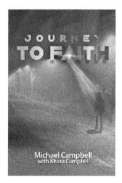

CPSIA information can be obtained
at www.ICGtesting.com
Printed in the USA
LVHW081152211020
669386LV00005B/857